Q & RAY

CASE #2
METEORITE OR METEOR-WRONG?

TRISHA SPEED SHASKAN

ILLUSTRATED BY STEPHEN SHASKAN

Graphic Universe™ • Minneapolis

Special thanks to Dr. Randy Korotev —TSS and SS

For my nephews Jude and Desmond, the brightest stars, for continually inspiring me. I love you so! —TSS

To Almeida Williams —SS

Graphic Universe™
A division of Lerner Publishing Group, Inc.
241 First Avenue North
Minneapolis, MN 55401 USA

For reading levels and more information, look up this title at www.lernerbooks.com.

Main body text set in CCDaveGibbonsLower 11.5/13.25.
Typeface provided by ComicCraft.

Library of Congress Cataloging-in-Publication Data

Names: Shaskan, Trisha Speed, 1973– author. | Shaskan, Stephen, illustrator.
Title: Meteorite or meteor-wrong! / written by Trisha Speed Shaskan ; illustrated by Stephen Shaskan.
Description: Minneapolis : Graphic Universe, [2018] | Series: Q & Ray ; case #2 | Summary: "Quillan Hedgeson, a hedgehog, and Raymond Ratzberg, a rat, are students (and crime solvers) at Elm Tree Elementary school. When a famous local meteorite goes missing, Q and Ray set out to solve the case, using their wits and a series of disguises" –Provided by publisher. | Includes bibliographical references. | Description based on print version record and CIP data provided by publisher; resource not viewed.
Identifiers: LCCN 2016037376 (print) | LCCN 2017016808 (ebook) | ISBN 9781512451221 (eb pdf) | ISBN 9781512411485 (lb : alk. paper)
Subjects: LCSH: Graphic novels. | CYAC: Graphic novels. | Mystery and detective stories. | Meteorites–Fiction. | Science museums–Fiction. | School field trips–Fiction. | Hedgehogs–Fiction. | Rats–Fiction.
Classification: LCC PZ7.7.S455 (ebook) | LCC PZ7.7.S455 Met 2018 (print) | DDC 741.5/973–dc23

LC record available at https://lccn.loc.gov/2016037376

Manufactured in the United States of America
1-39654-21286-8/2/2017

WHO'S WHO

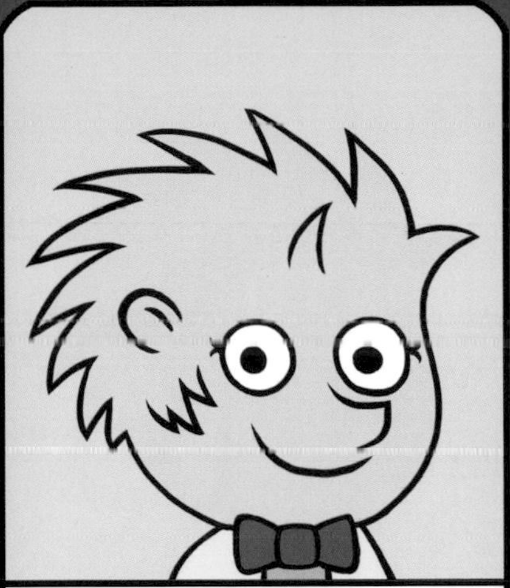

Quillan Hedgeson
aka: Q

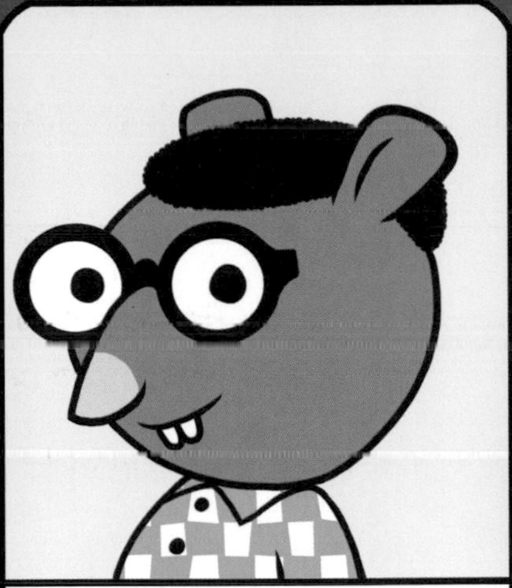

Ray Ratzberg

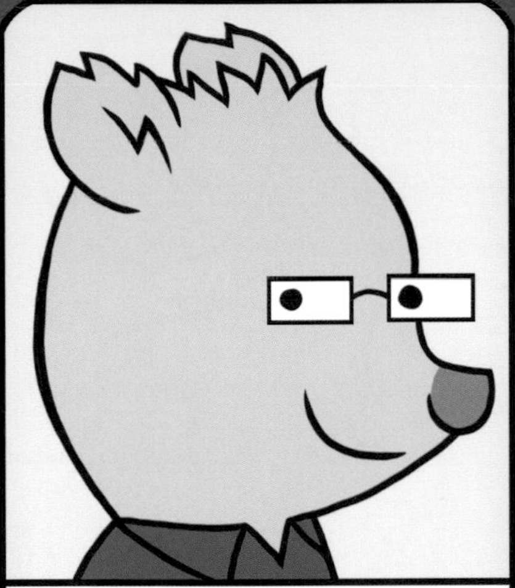

Mr. Shrew
Media Specialist

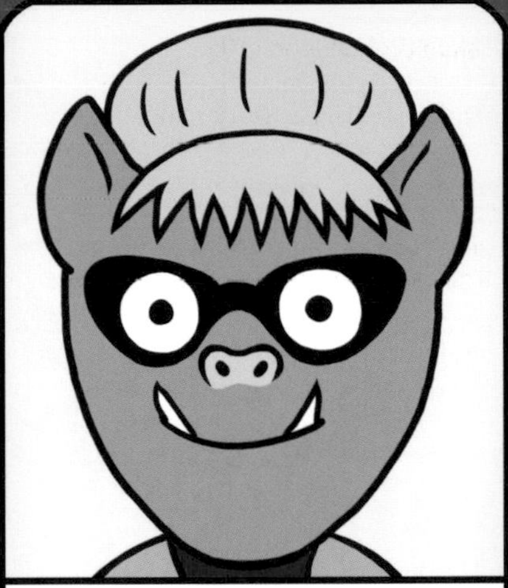

Ms. Boar
Classroom Teacher

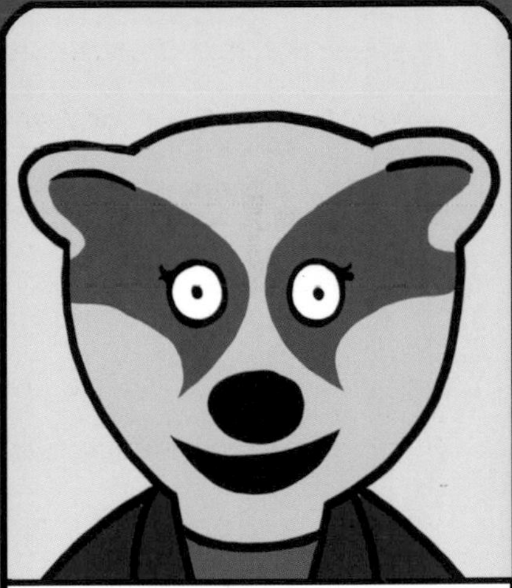

Principal Badger

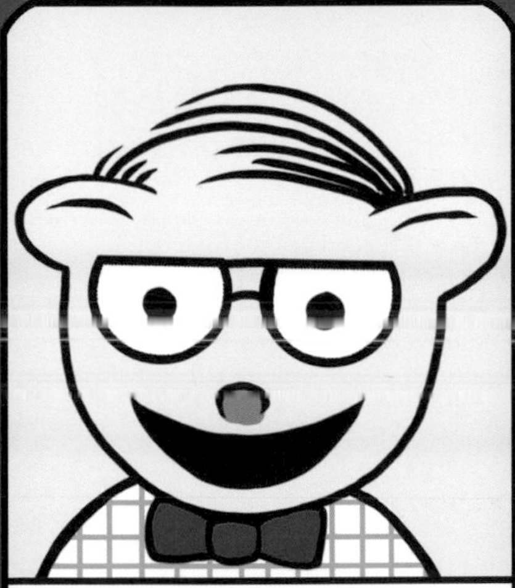

Frank Ferret

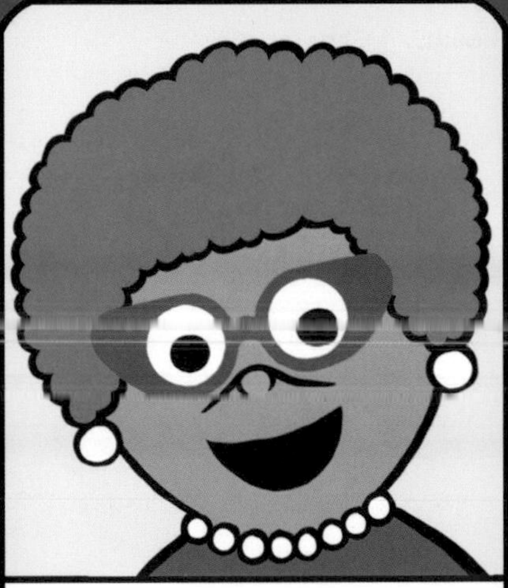

Ms. Mole

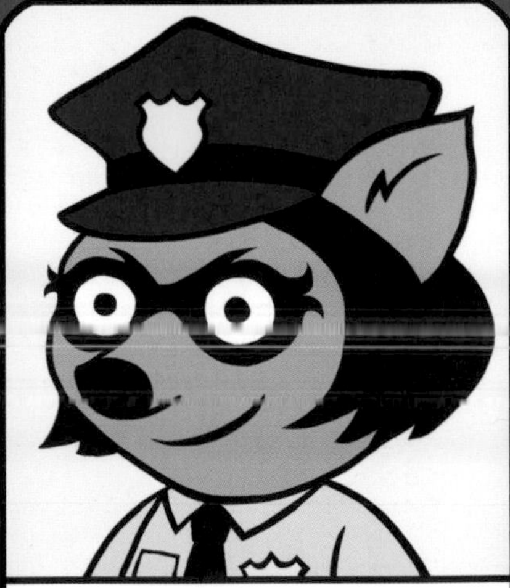

Officer Rocco

CHAPTER ONE

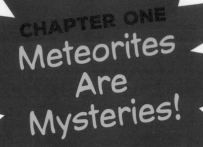

Meteorites Are Mysteries!

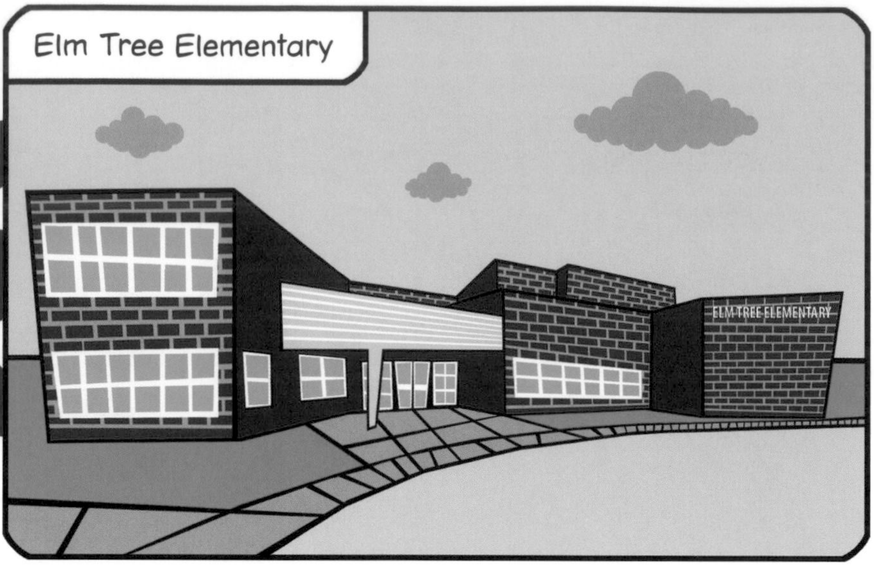
Elm Tree Elementary
ELM TREE ELEMENTARY

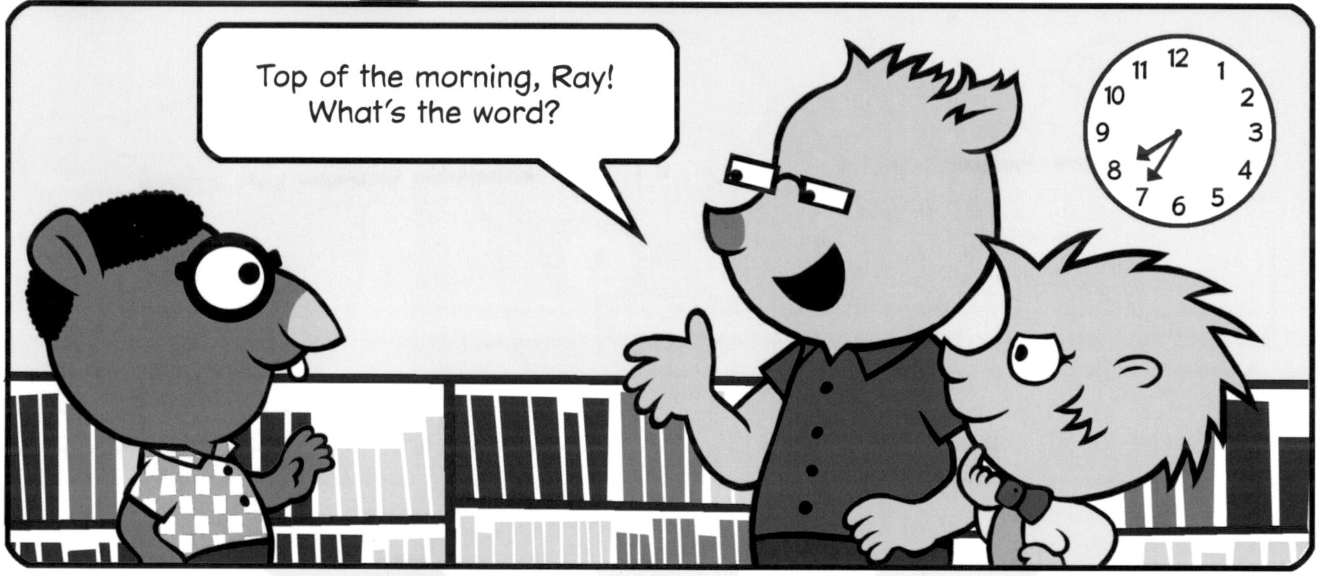
Top of the morning, Ray! What's the word?

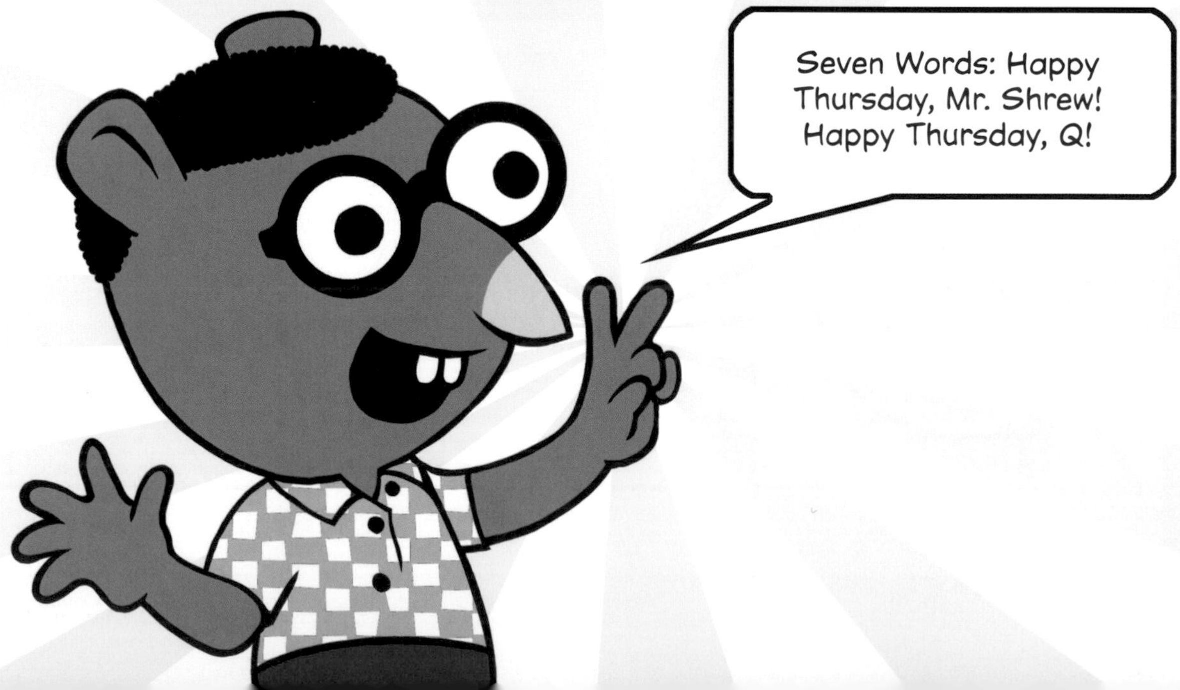
Seven Words: Happy Thursday, Mr. Shrew! Happy Thursday, Q!

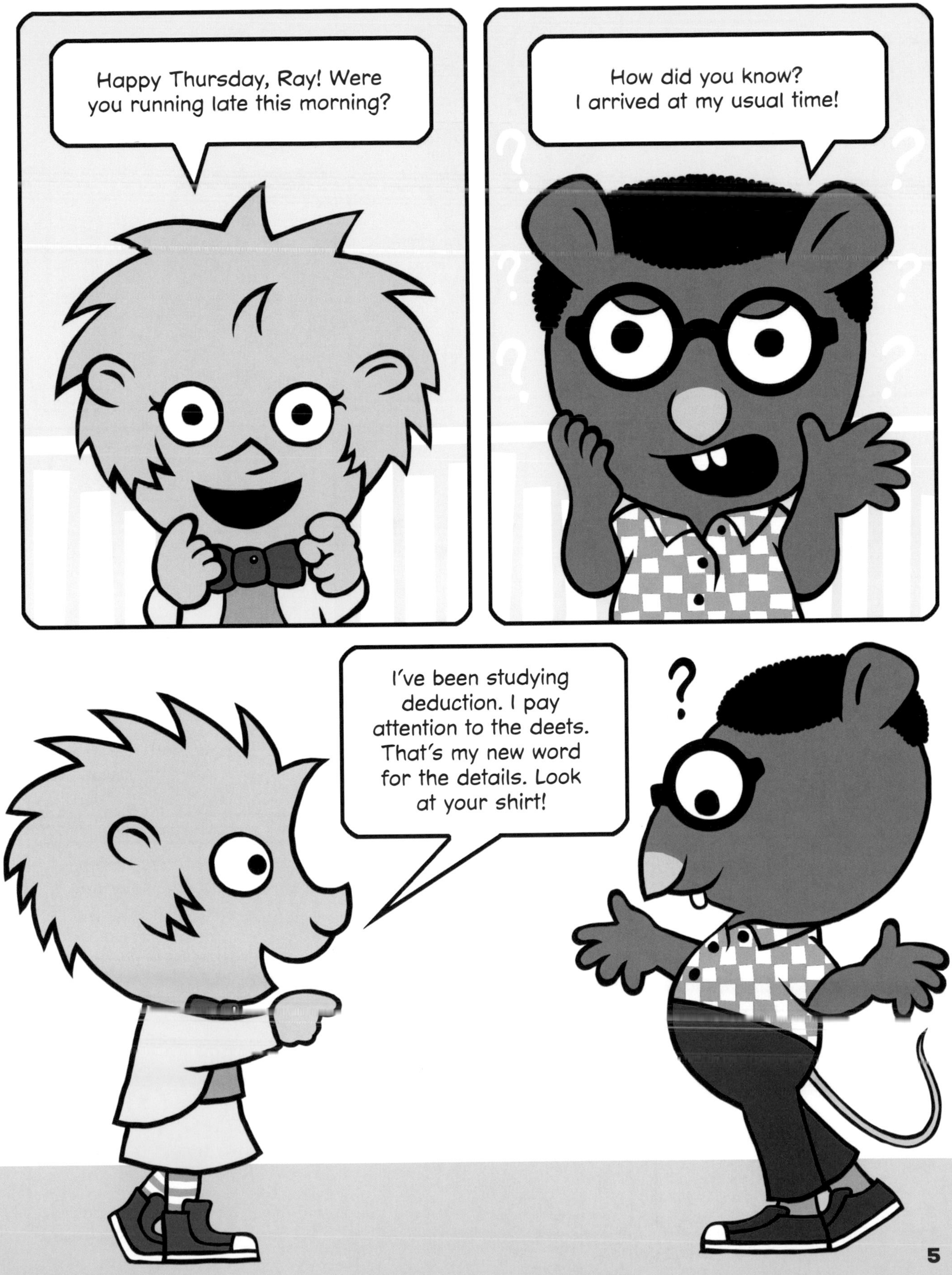
Happy Thursday, Ray! Were you running late this morning?
How did you know? I arrived at my usual time!
I've been studying deduction. I pay attention to the deets. That's my new word for the details. Look at your shirt!

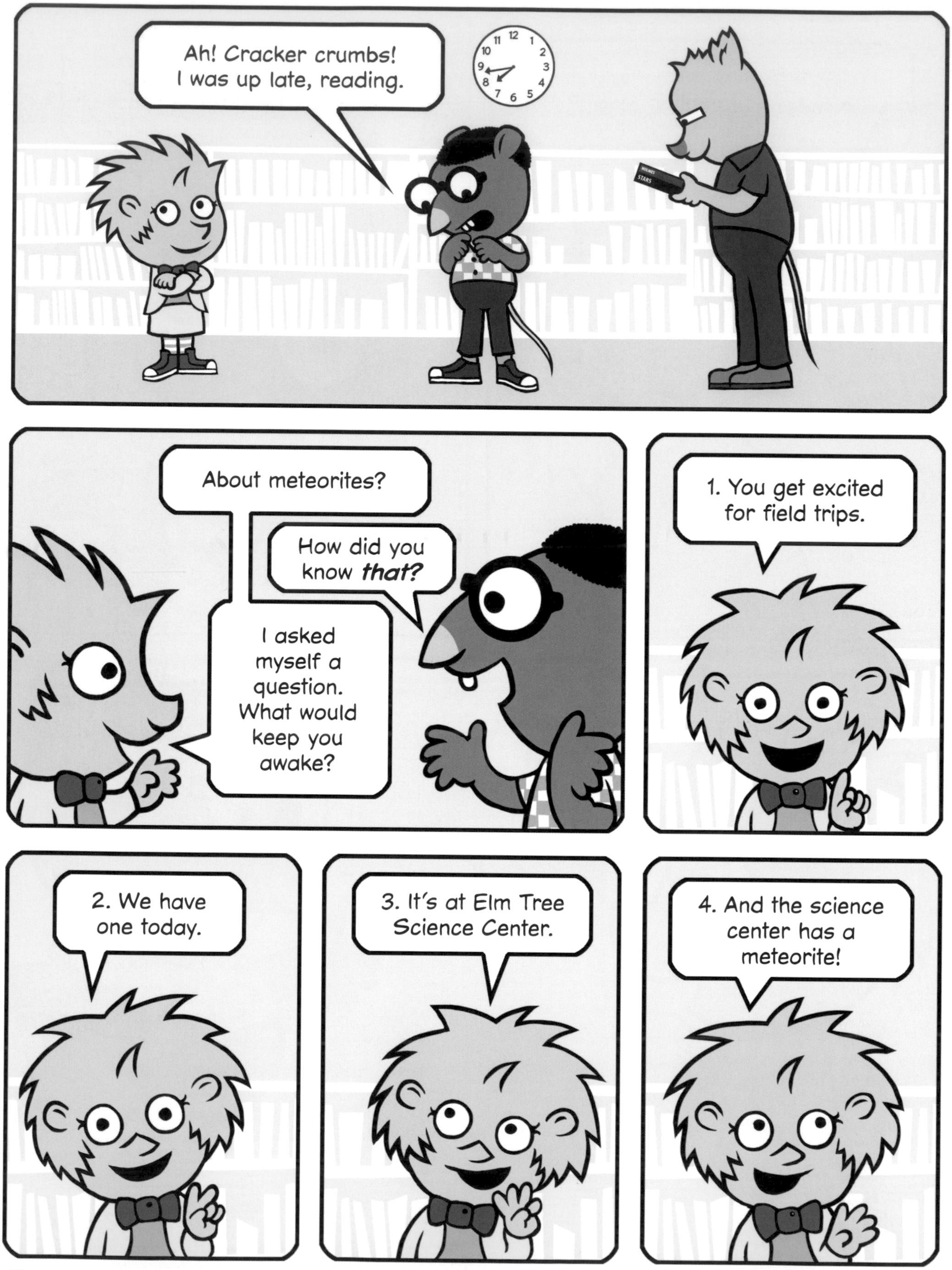

Ah! Cracker crumbs! I was up late, reading.
About meteorites?
How did you know *that?*
I asked myself a question. What would keep you awake?
1. You get excited for field trips.
2. We have one today.
3. It's at Elm Tree Science Center.
4. And the science center has a meteorite!

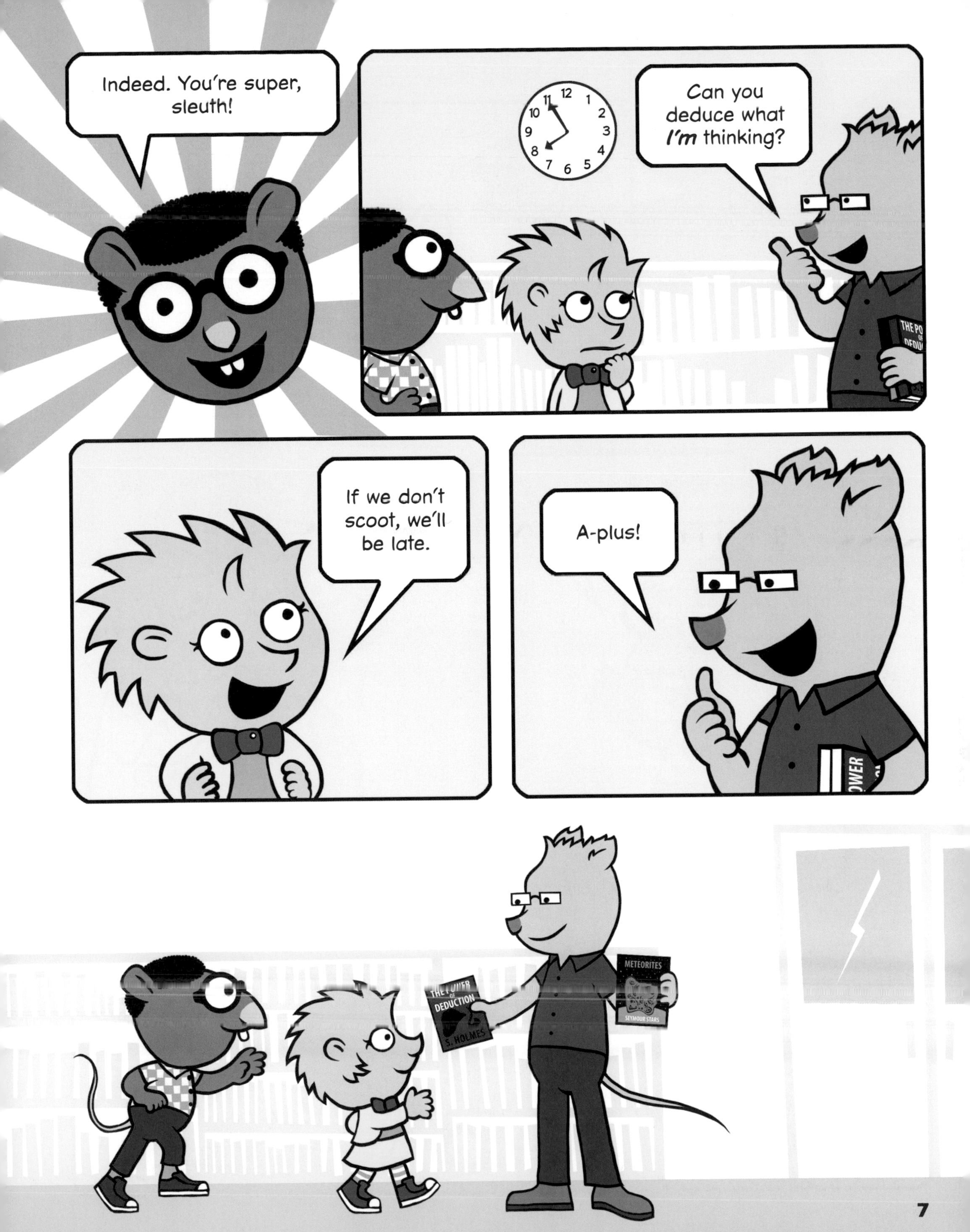
Indeed. You're super, sleuth!
Can you deduce what *I'm* thinking?
If we don't scoot, we'll be late.
A-plus!
THE POWER OF DEDUCTION
S. HOLMES
METEORITES
SEYMOUR STARS

CHAPTER TWO
Meet Frank Ferret

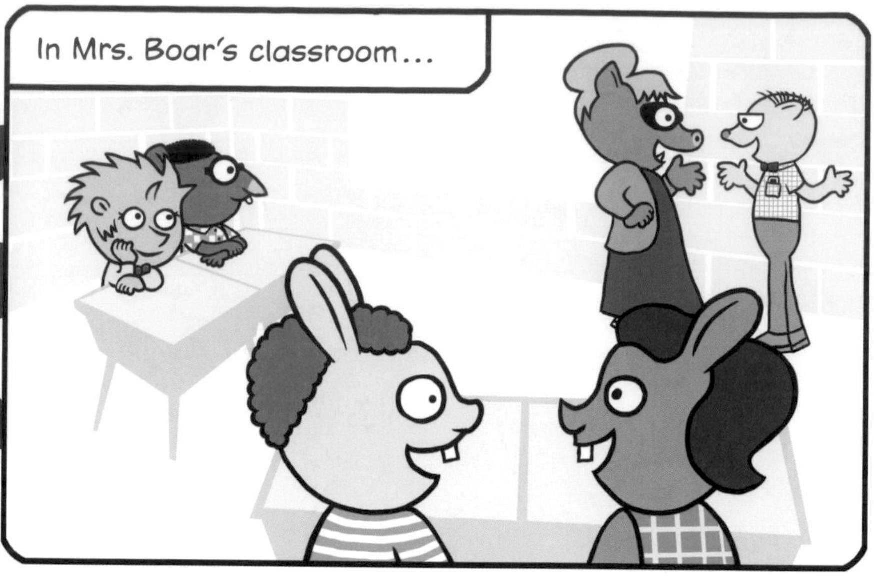
In Mrs. Boar's classroom...

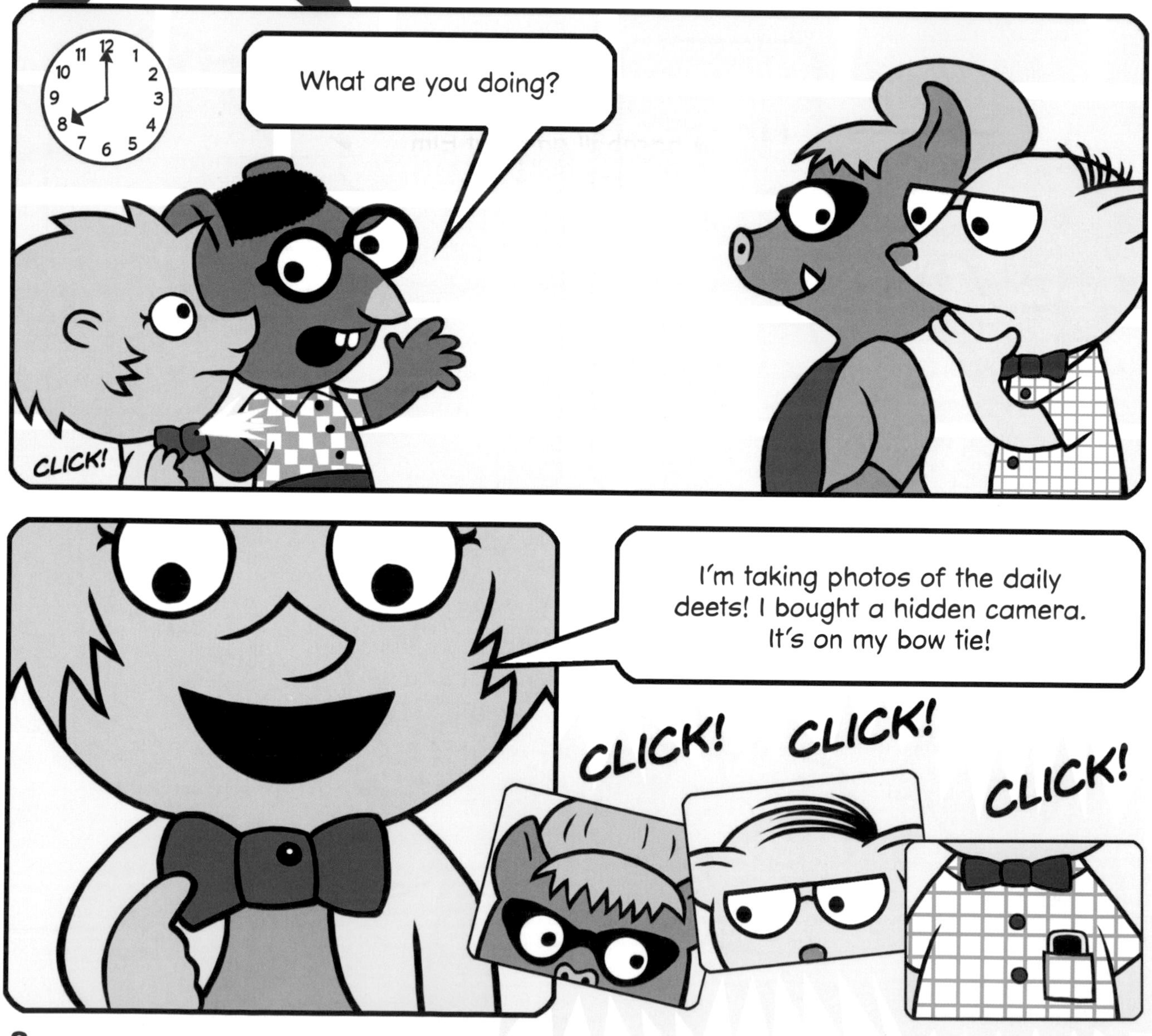
What are you doing?
CLICK!
I'm taking photos of the daily deets! I bought a hidden camera. It's on my bow tie!
CLICK!
CLICK!
CLICK!

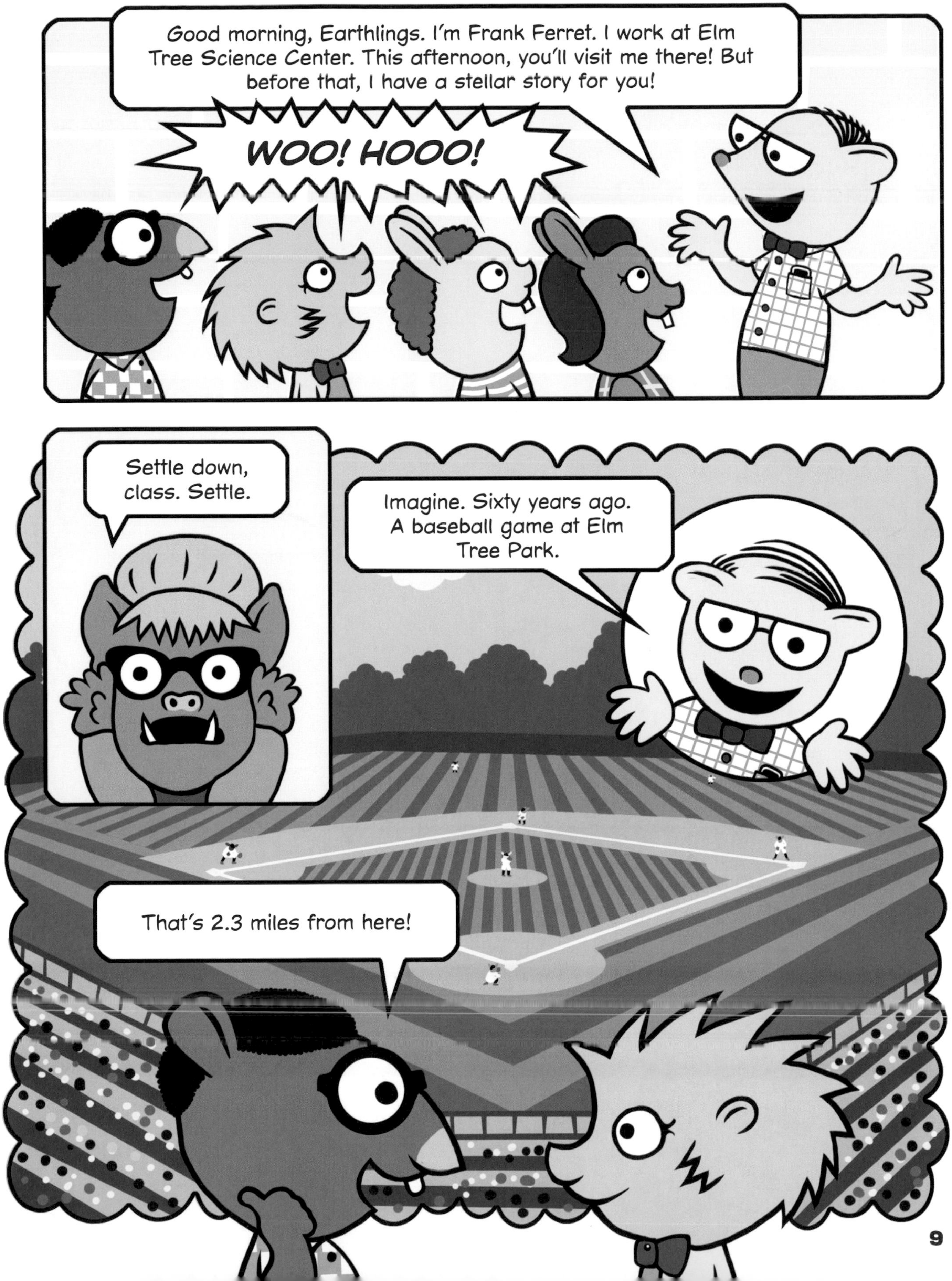
Good morning, Earthlings. I'm Frank Ferret. I work at Elm Tree Science Center. This afternoon, you'll visit me there! But before that, I have a stellar story for you!
WOO! HOOO!
Settle down, class. Settle.
Imagine. Sixty years ago. A baseball game at Elm Tree Park.
That's 2.3 miles from here!

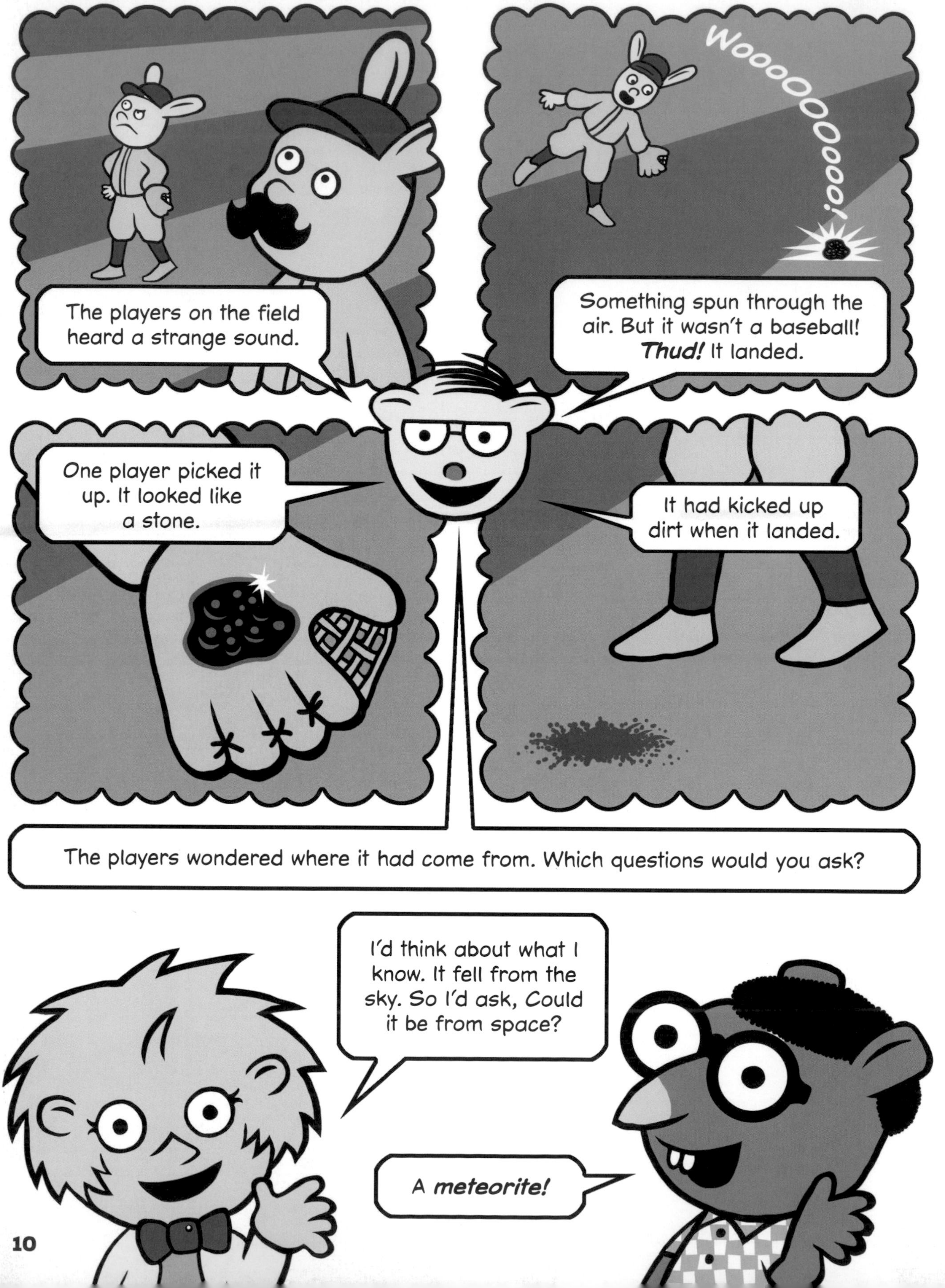
The players on the field heard a strange sound.
WoooOOOOoooo!
Something spun through the air. But it wasn't a baseball! *Thud!* It landed.
One player picked it up. It looked like a stone.
It had kicked up dirt when it landed.
The players wondered where it had come from. Which questions would you ask?
I'd think about what I know. It fell from the sky. So I'd ask, Could it be from space?
A *meteorite!*

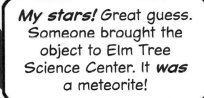

My stars! Great guess. Someone brought the object to Elm Tree Science Center. It *was* a meteorite!

Ms. Boar, can you turn off the lights?

CLICK!

METEORITES AND YOU!

Space is full of rocks.

BANG! BANG! Big rocks bump around until they break into smaller pieces.

Sometimes a piece enters Earth's atmosphere. That's a layer of gases around Earth.

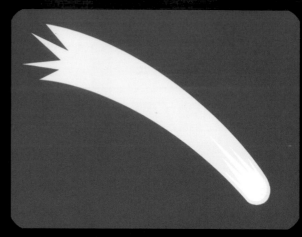

The space rock speeds through the atmosphere. The thin outer layer of the rock heats up and melts off.

The melting part becomes the tail. It looks like a streak of light. It's called a meteor!

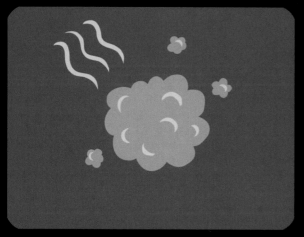

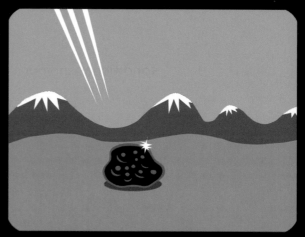

Sometimes the rest of the space rock burns up.

Sometimes it lands on Earth! *THUMP!* Now the rock is called a meteorite. Later, you'll get to see the one that landed in Elm Tree Park!

Woo! Hoo! Aaaah!

Cool! Yay!

CHAPTER THREE
Limburger-Rite or Limburger-Wrong?

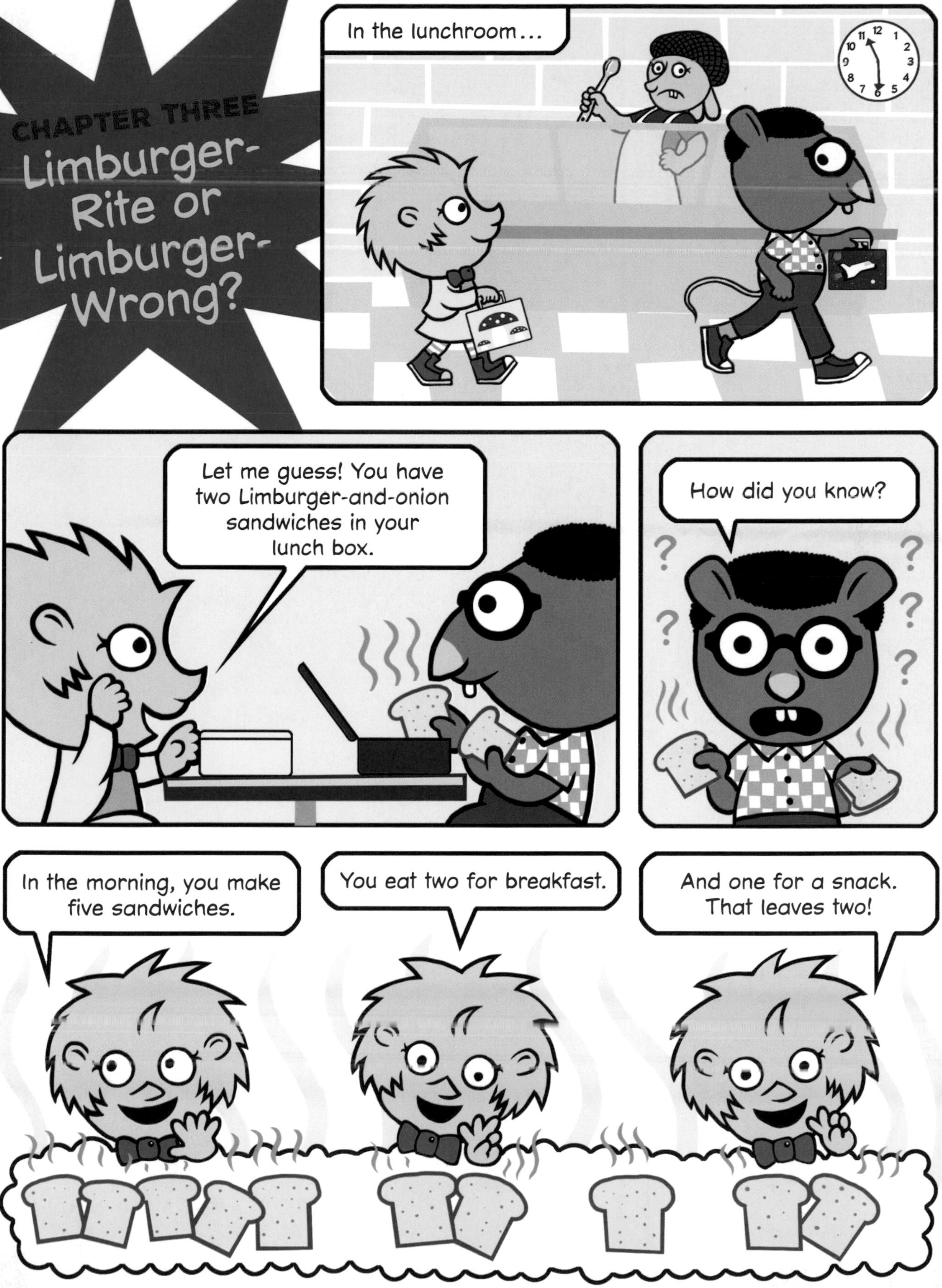
In the lunchroom…
Let me guess! You have two Limburger-and-onion sandwiches in your lunch box.
How did you know?
In the morning, you make five sandwiches.
You eat two for breakfast.
And one for a snack. That leaves two!

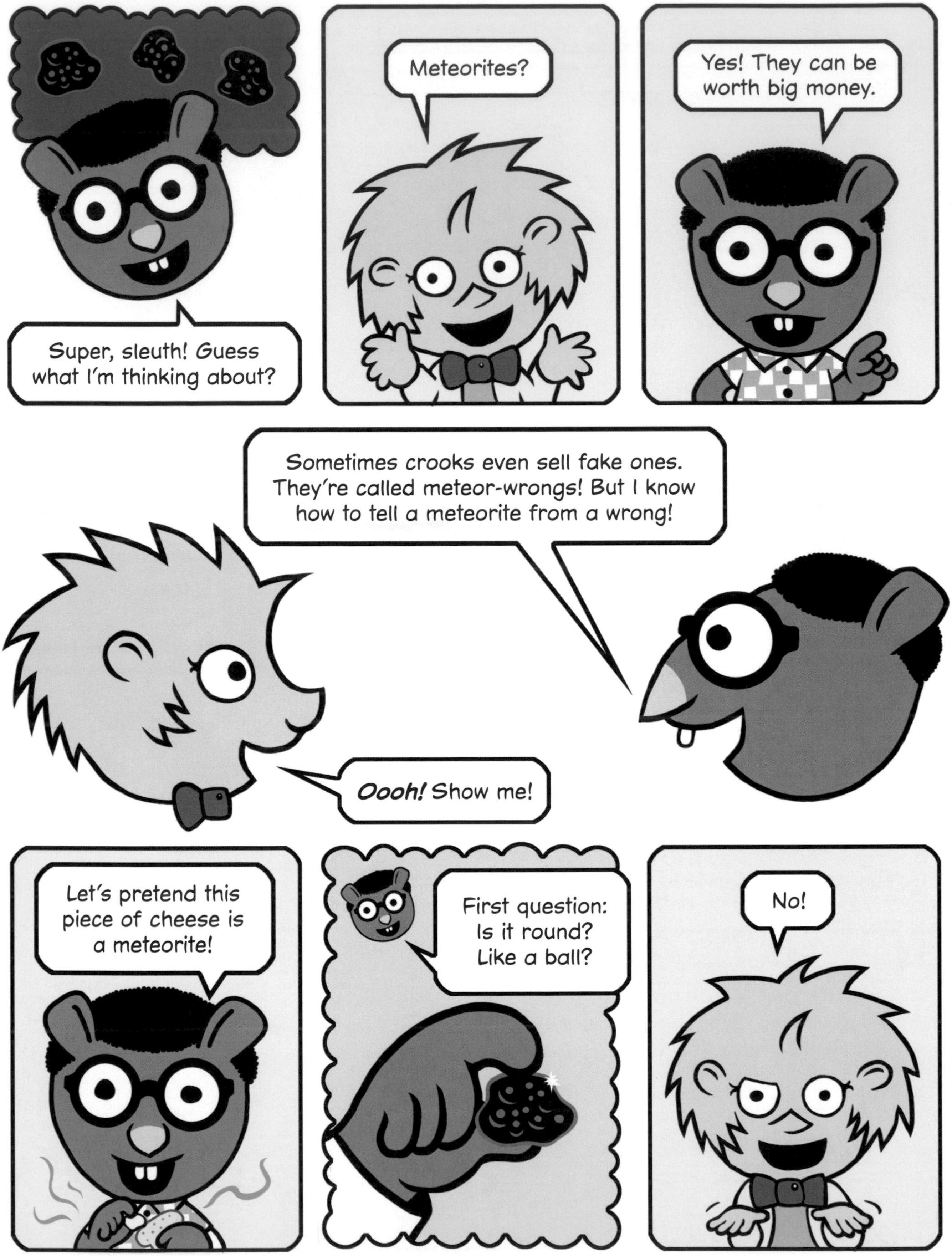
Super, sleuth! Guess what I'm thinking about?
Meteorites?
Yes! They can be worth big money.
Sometimes crooks even sell fake ones. They're called meteor-wrongs! But I know how to tell a meteorite from a wrong!
Oooh! Show me!
Let's pretend this piece of cheese is a meteorite!
First question: Is it round? Like a ball?
No!

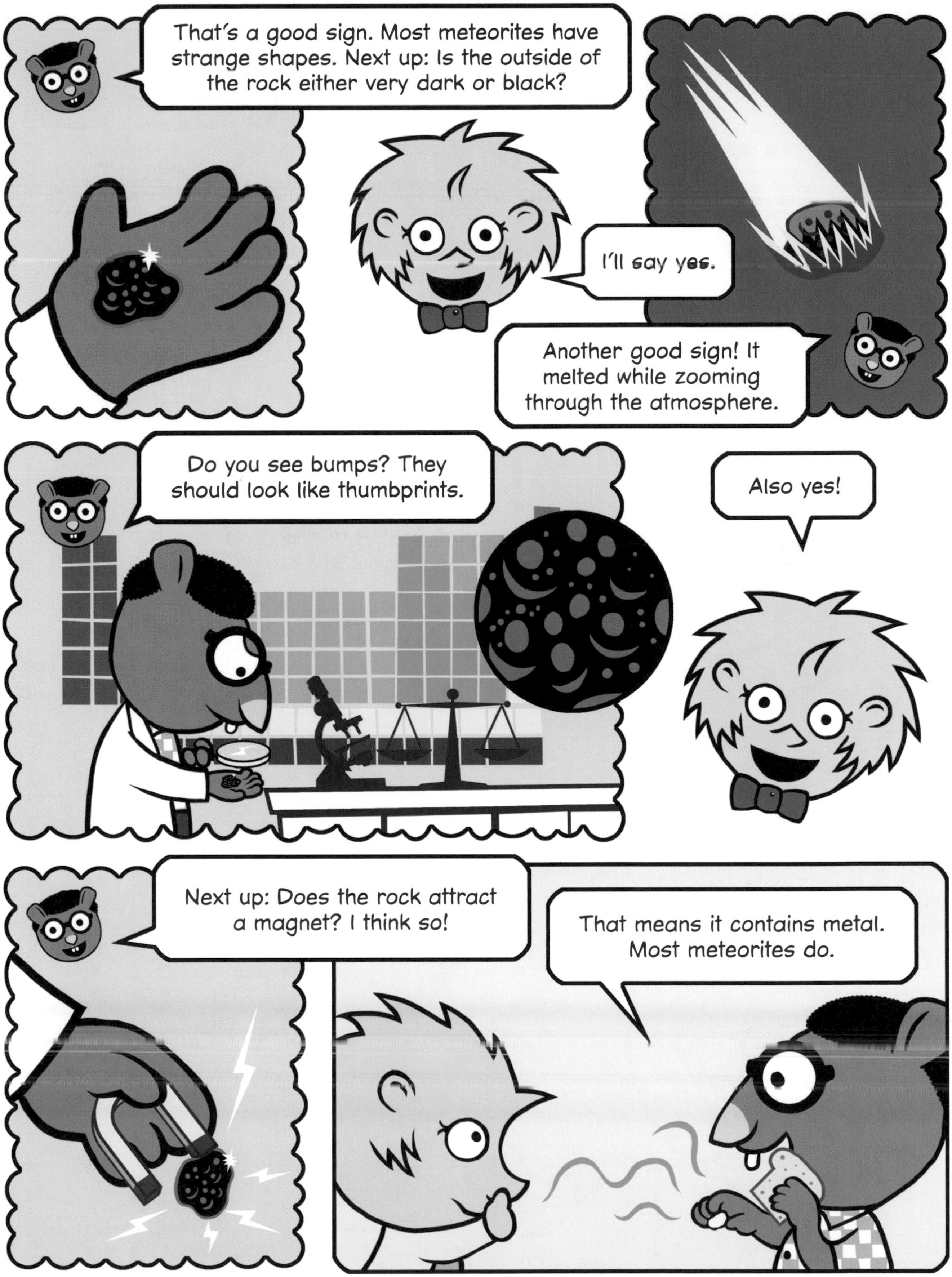
That's a good sign. Most meteorites have strange shapes. Next up: Is the outside of the rock either very dark or black?
I'll say yes.
Another good sign! It melted while zooming through the atmosphere.
Do you see bumps? They should look like thumbprints.
Also yes!
Next up: Does the rock attract a magnet? I think so!
That means it contains metal. Most meteorites do.

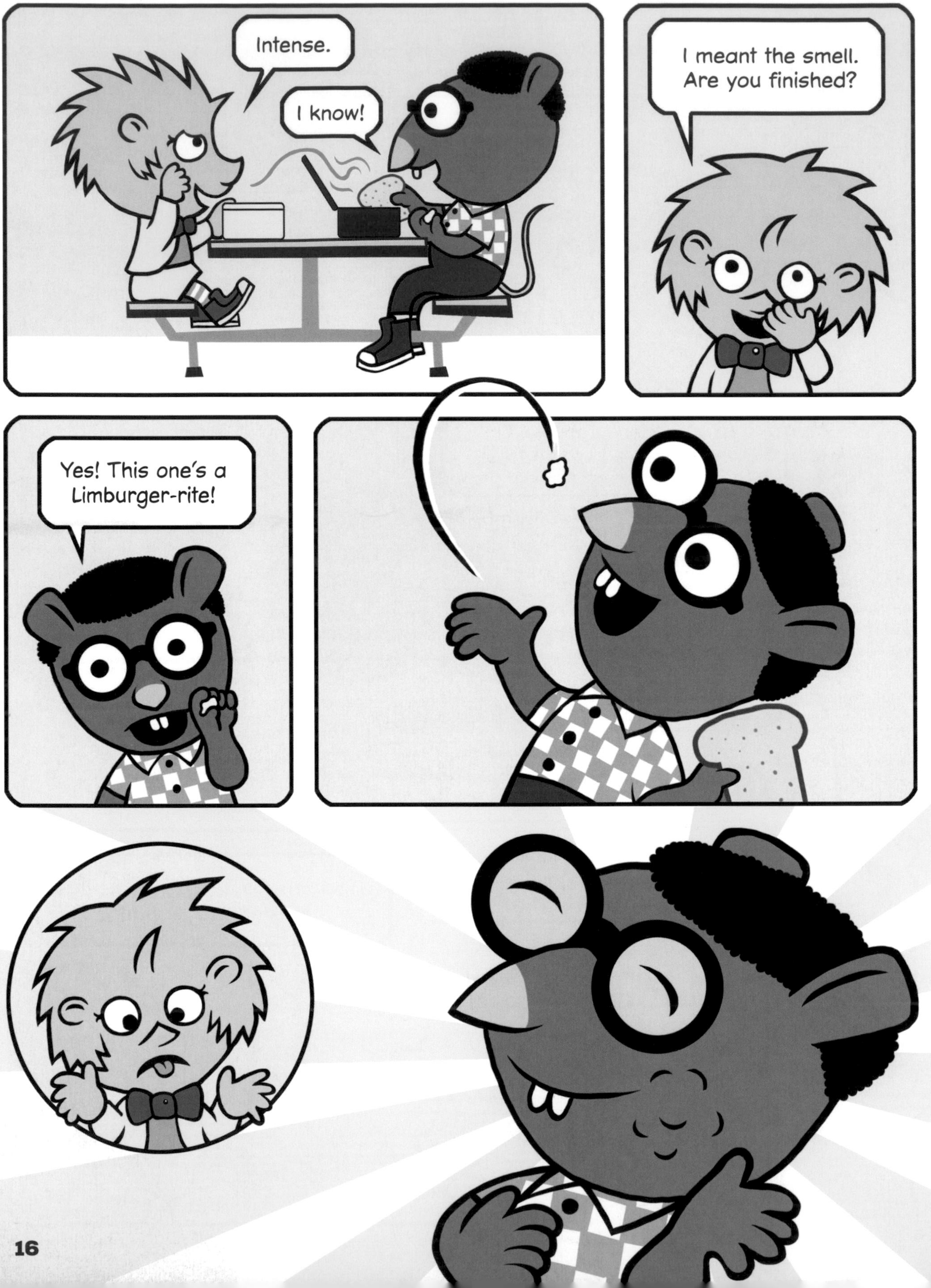
Intense.
I know!
I meant the smell. Are you finished?
Yes! This one's a Limburger-rite!

CHAPTER FOUR
The Elm Tree Park Meteorite

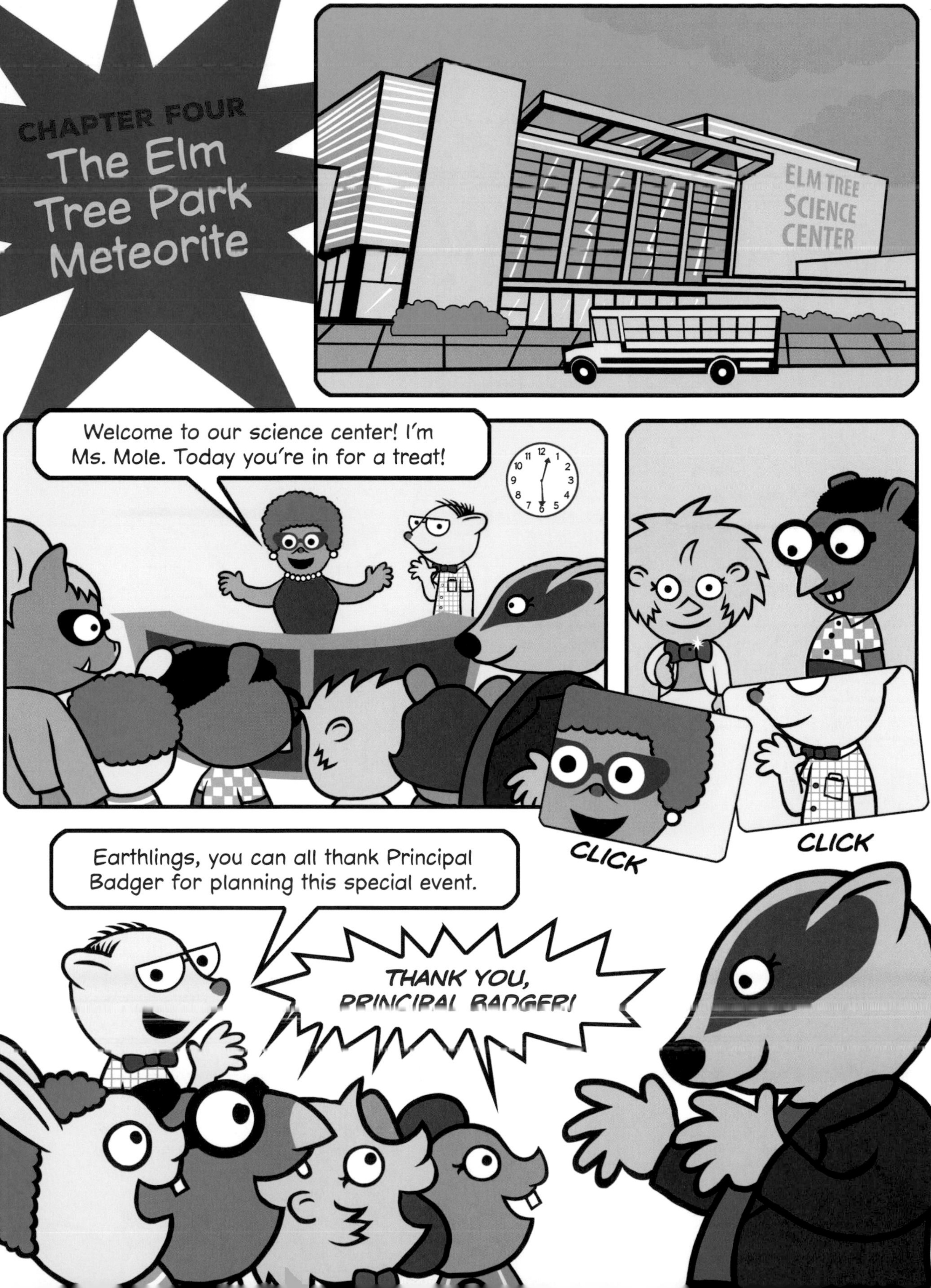
ELM TREE SCIENCE CENTER
Welcome to our science center! I'm Ms. Mole. Today you're in for a treat!
CLICK
CLICK
Earthlings, you can all thank Principal Badger for planning this special event.
THANK YOU, PRINCIPAL BADGER!

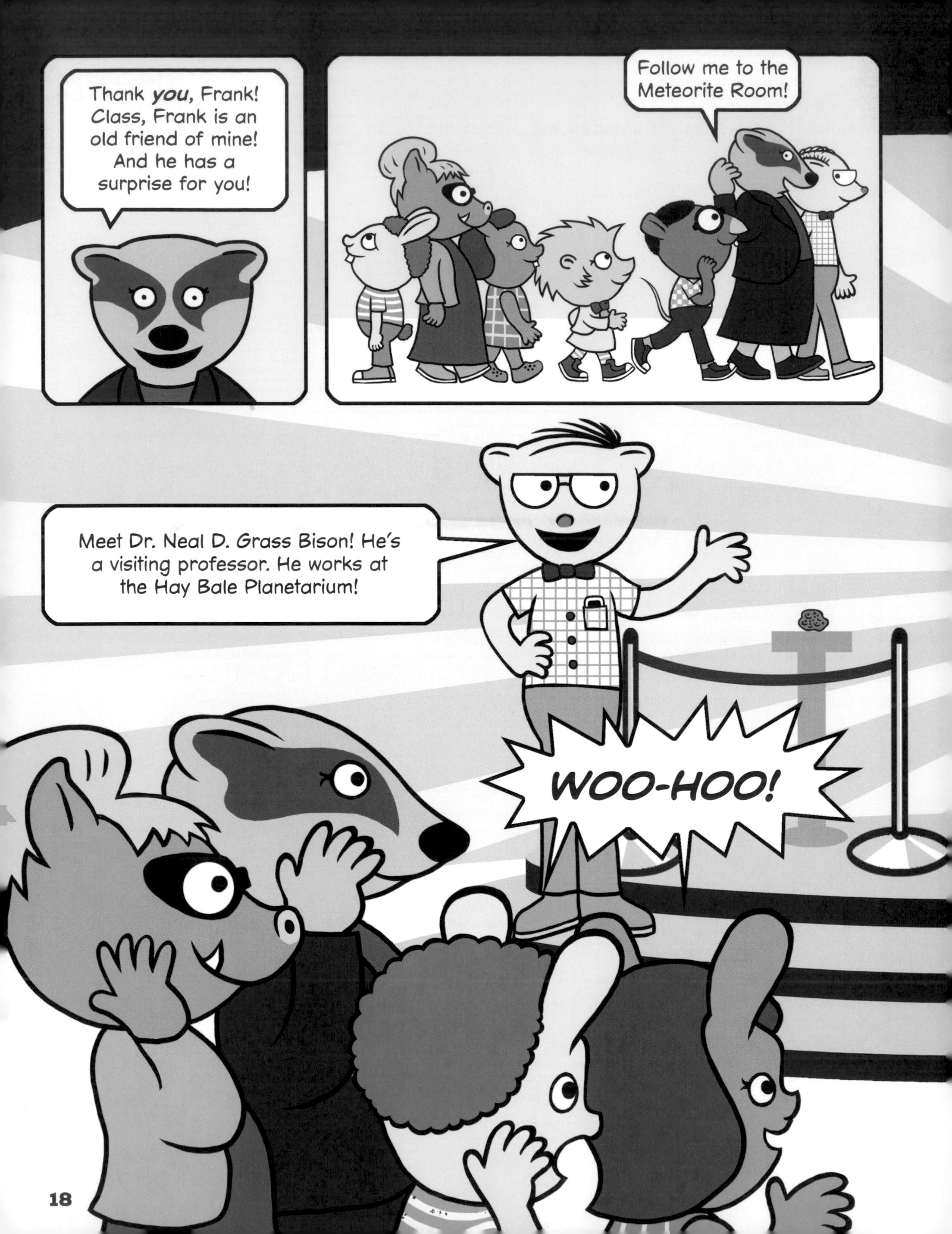
Thank *you*, Frank! Class, Frank is an old friend of mine! And he has a surprise for you!
Follow me to the Meteorite Room!
Meet Dr. Neal D. Grass Bison! He's a visiting professor. He works at the Hay Bale Planetarium!
WOO-HOO!

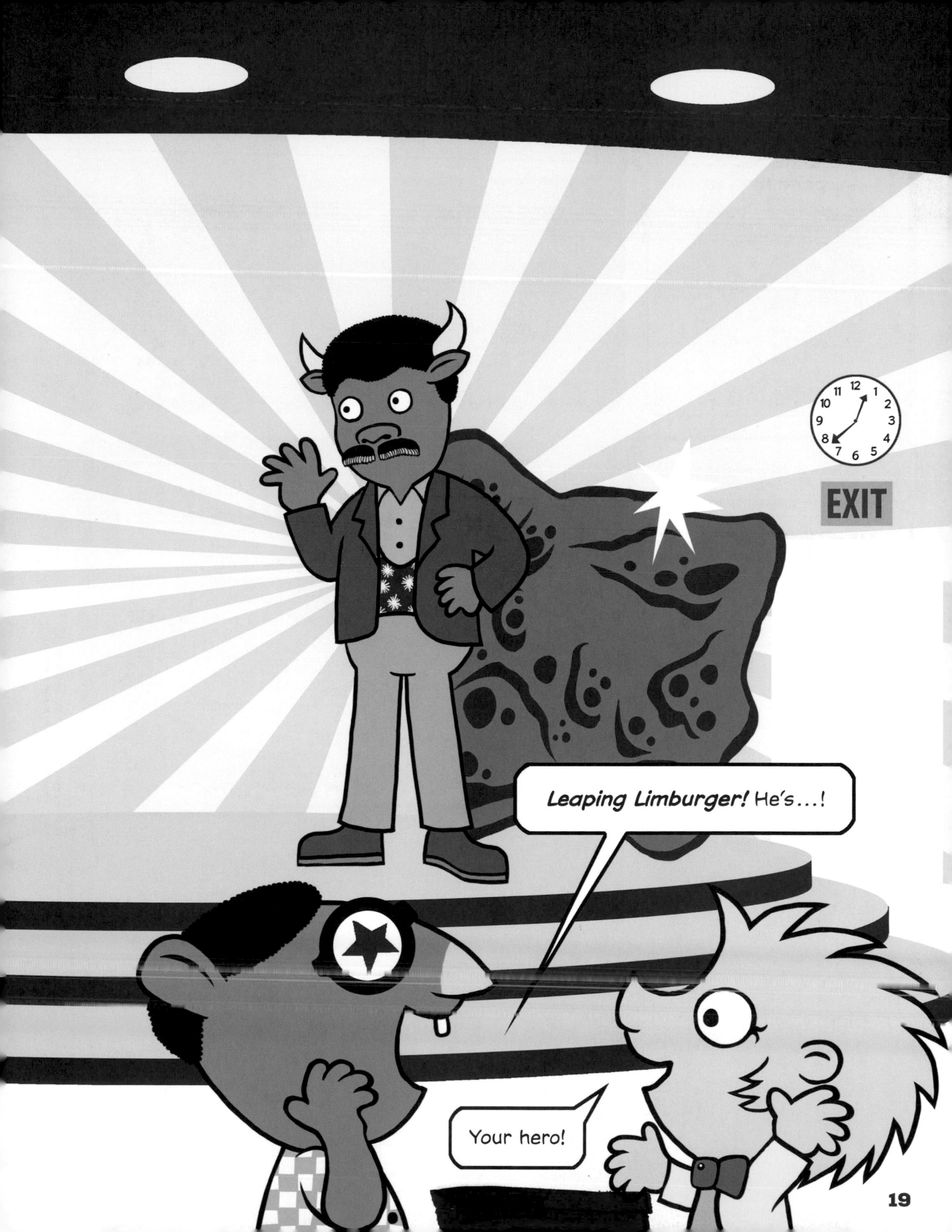
EXIT
Leaping Limburger! He's...!
Your hero!

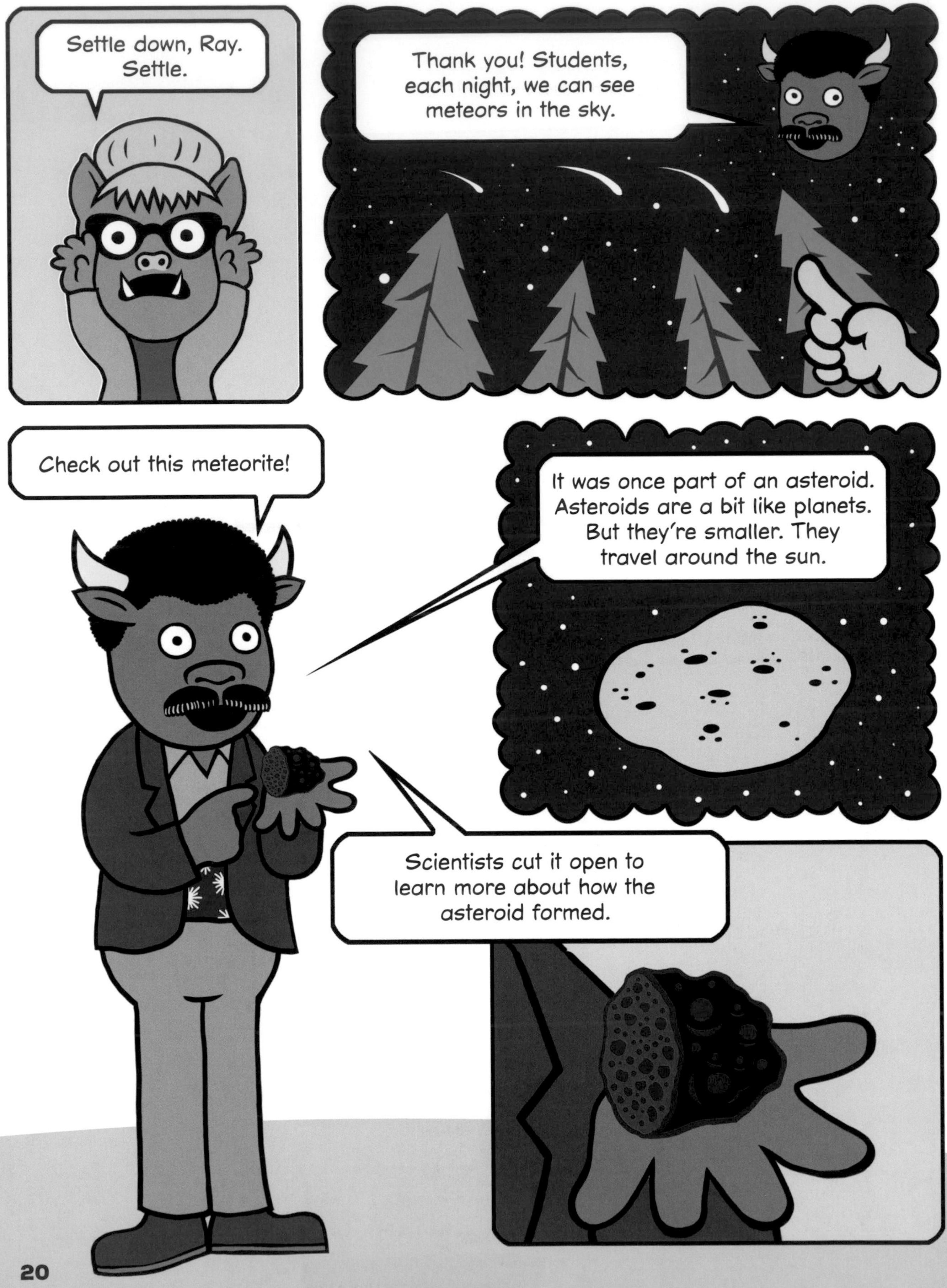
Settle down, Ray. Settle.
Thank you! Students, each night, we can see meteors in the sky.
Check out this meteorite!
It was once part of an asteroid. Asteroids are a bit like planets. But they're smaller. They travel around the sun.
Scientists cut it open to learn more about how the asteroid formed.

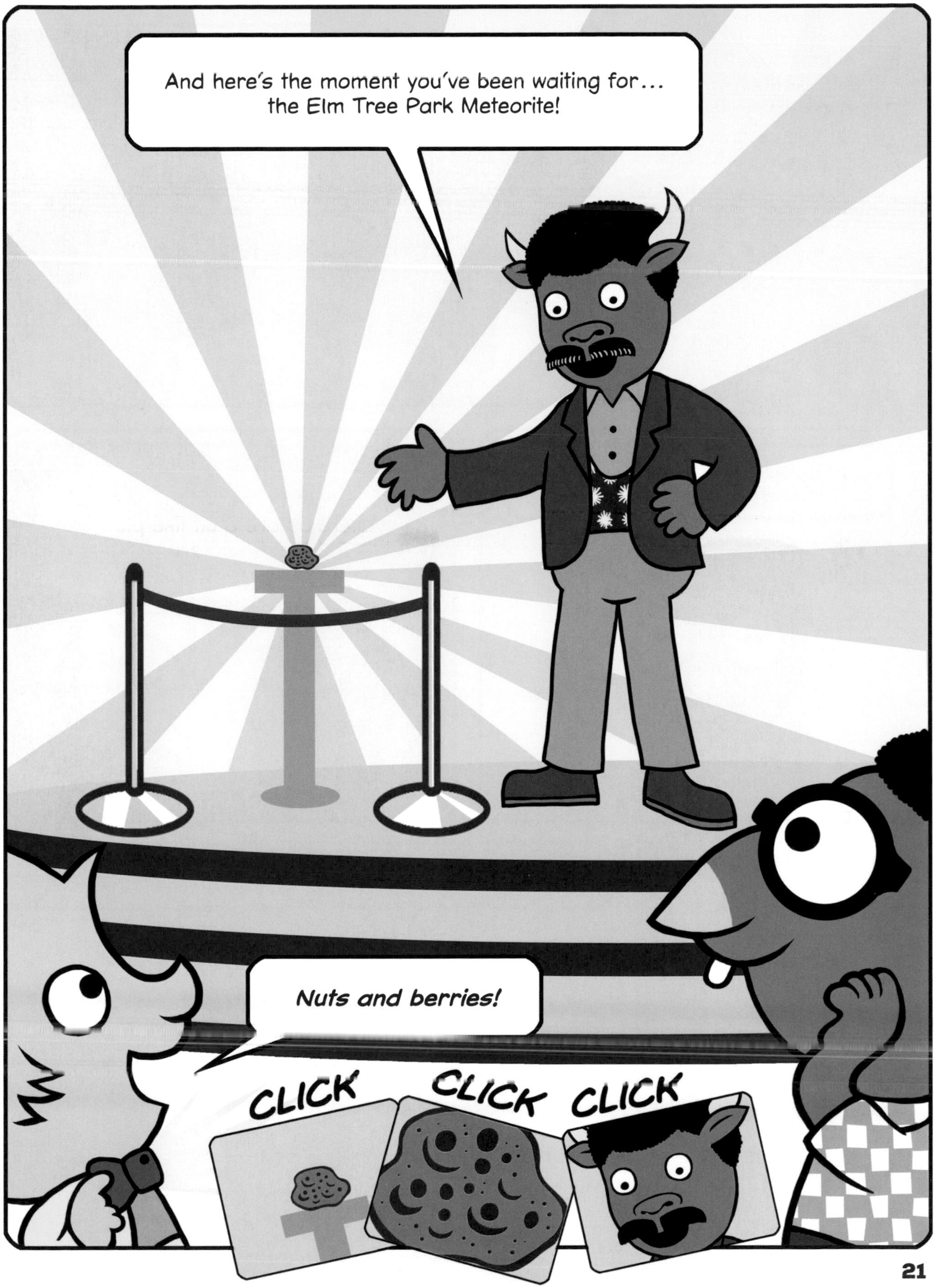
And here's the moment you've been waiting for...
the Elm Tree Park Meteorite!
Nuts and berries!
CLICK
CLICK
CLICK

CHAPTER FIVE

Meteorite or Meteor-Wrong?

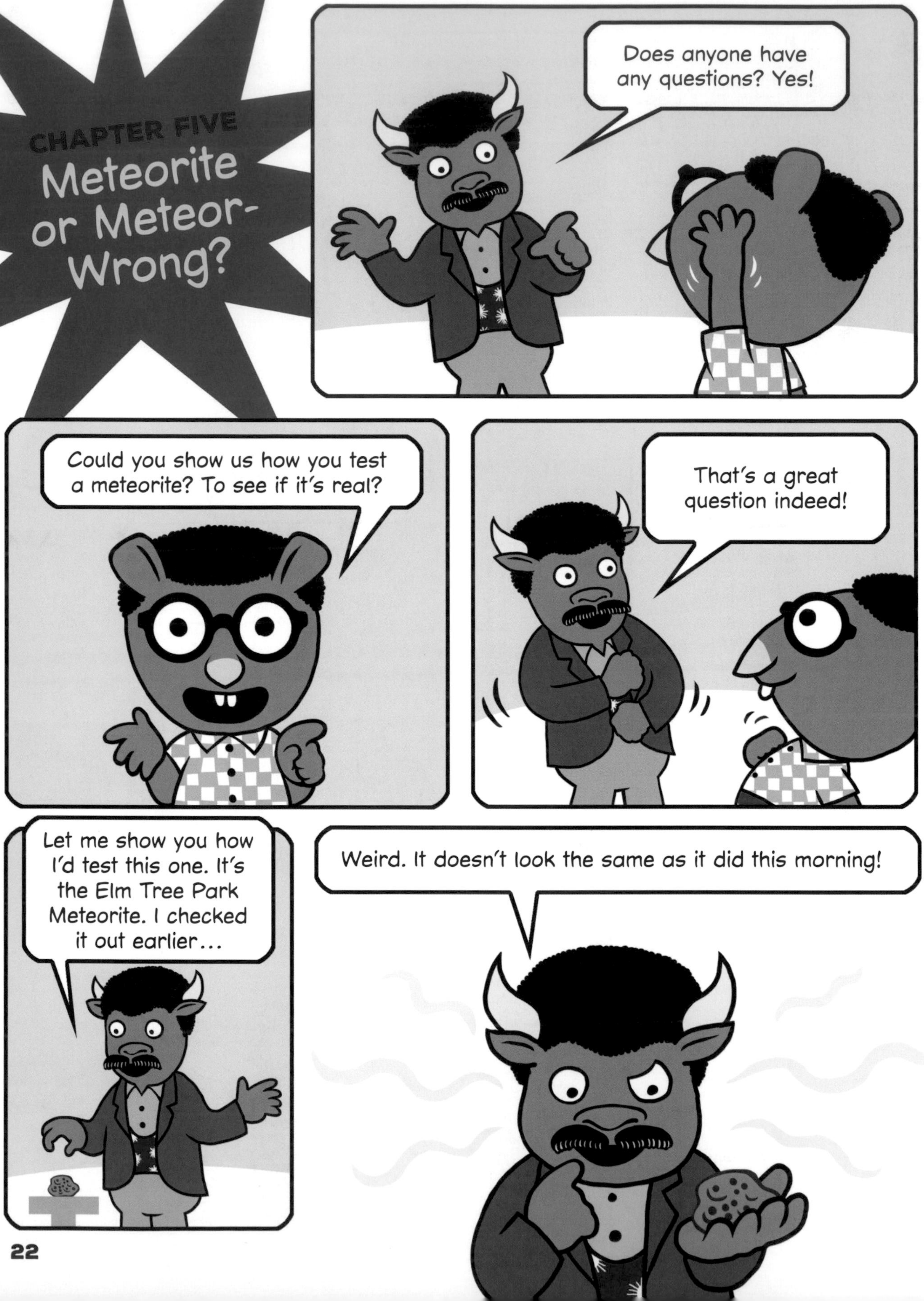
Does anyone have any questions? Yes!
Could you show us how you test a meteorite? To see if it's real?
That's a great question indeed!
Let me show you how I'd test this one. It's the Elm Tree Park Meteorite. I checked it out earlier...
Weird. It doesn't look the same as it did this morning!

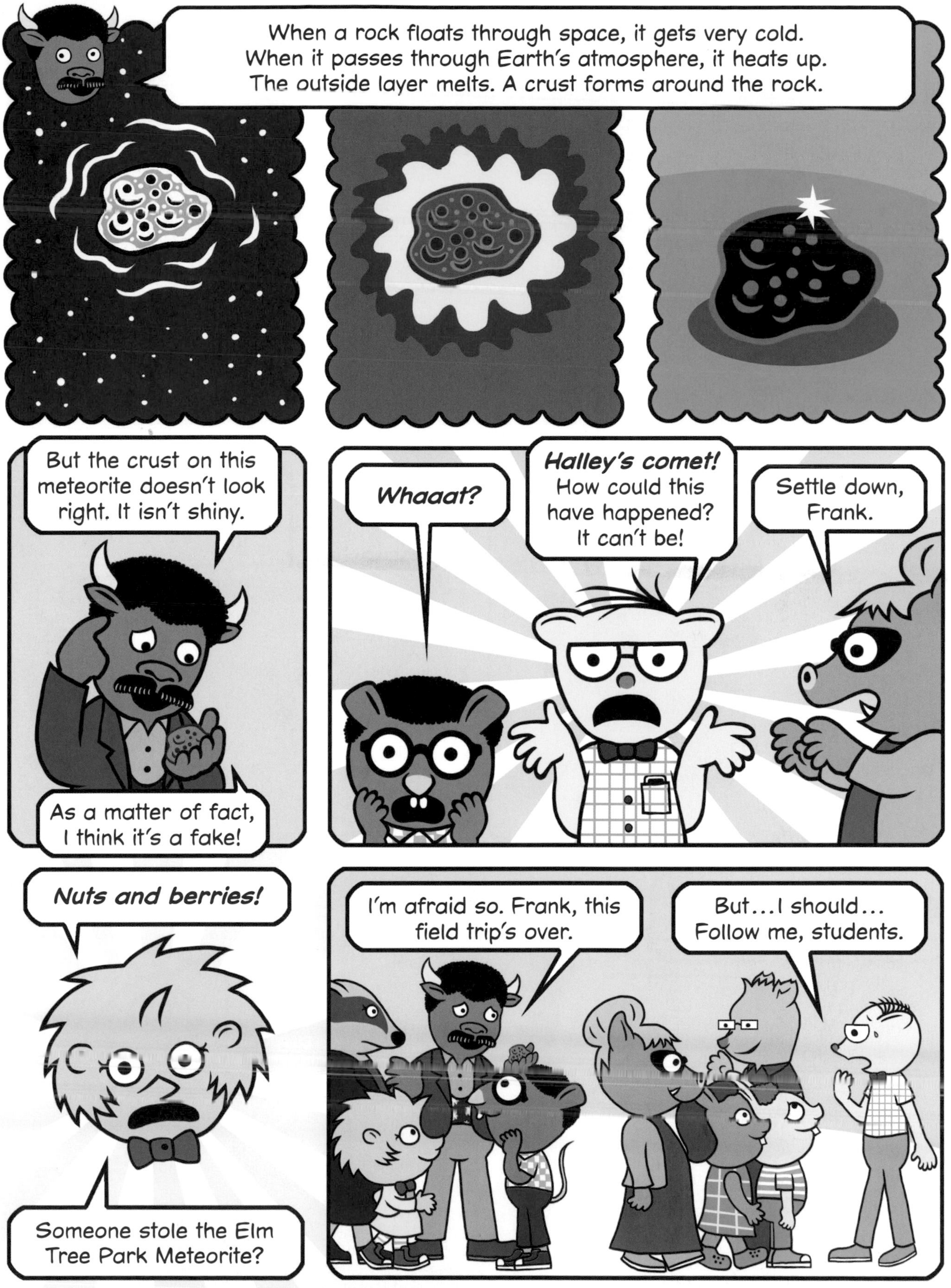

When a rock floats through space, it gets very cold. When it passes through Earth's atmosphere, it heats up. The outside layer melts. A crust forms around the rock.
But the crust on this meteorite doesn't look right. It isn't shiny.
As a matter of fact, I think it's a fake!
Whaaat?
Halley's comet! How could this have happened? It can't be!
Settle down, Frank.
Nuts and berries!
Someone stole the Elm Tree Park Meteorite?
I'm afraid so. Frank, this field trip's over.
But...I should... Follow me, students.

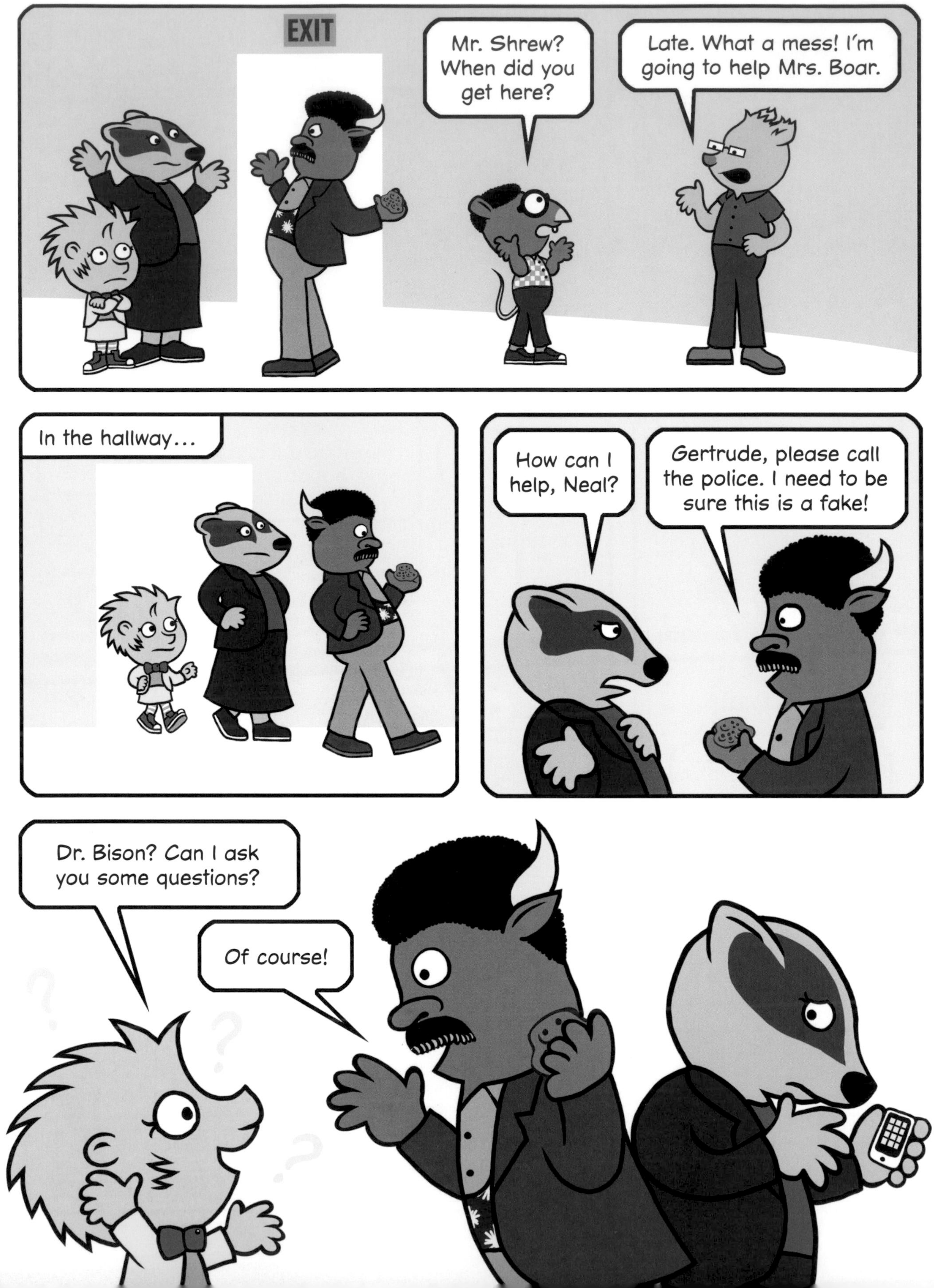
EXIT
Mr. Shrew? When did you get here?
Late. What a mess! I'm going to help Mrs. Boar.
In the hallway...
How can I help, Neal?
Gertrude, please call the police. I need to be sure this is a fake!
Dr. Bison? Can I ask you some questions?
Of course!

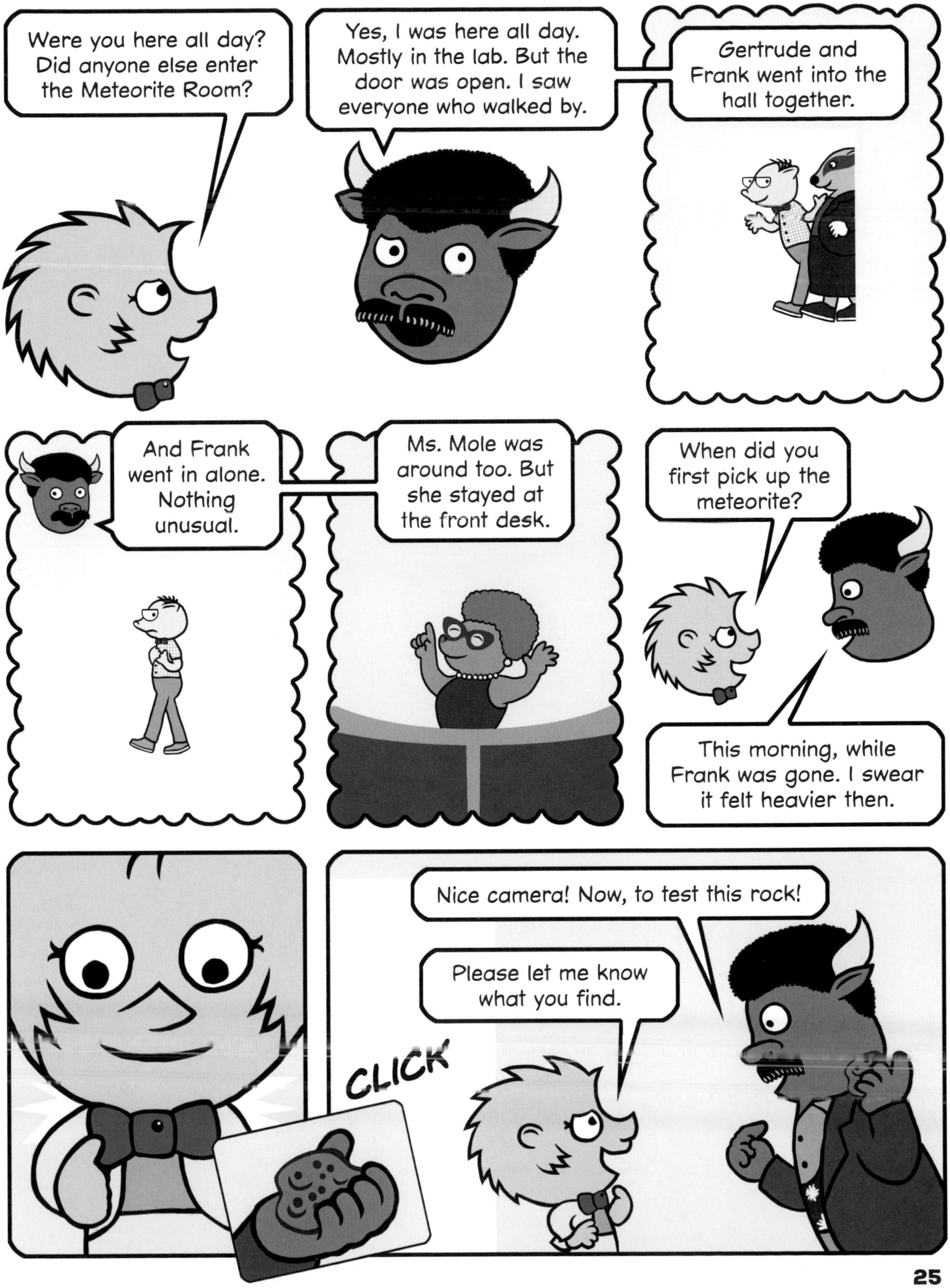

Were you here all day? Did anyone else enter the Meteorite Room?
Yes, I was here all day. Mostly in the lab. But the door was open. I saw everyone who walked by.
Gertrude and Frank went into the hall together.
And Frank went in alone. Nothing unusual.
Ms. Mole was around too. But she stayed at the front desk.
When did you first pick up the meteorite?
This morning, while Frank was gone. I swear it felt heavier then.
CLICK
Nice camera! Now, to test this rock!
Please let me know what you find.

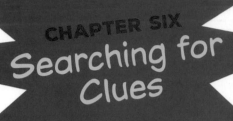

CHAPTER SIX
Searching for Clues

In the Meteorite Room...

EXIT

Leaping Limburger!

Can I help you?

Ms. Mole, were you at the desk all day? Who came and went? At what times?

Whoa! Slow down, Little Hedgie.

The name is Hedgeson. Quillan Lu Hedgeson.

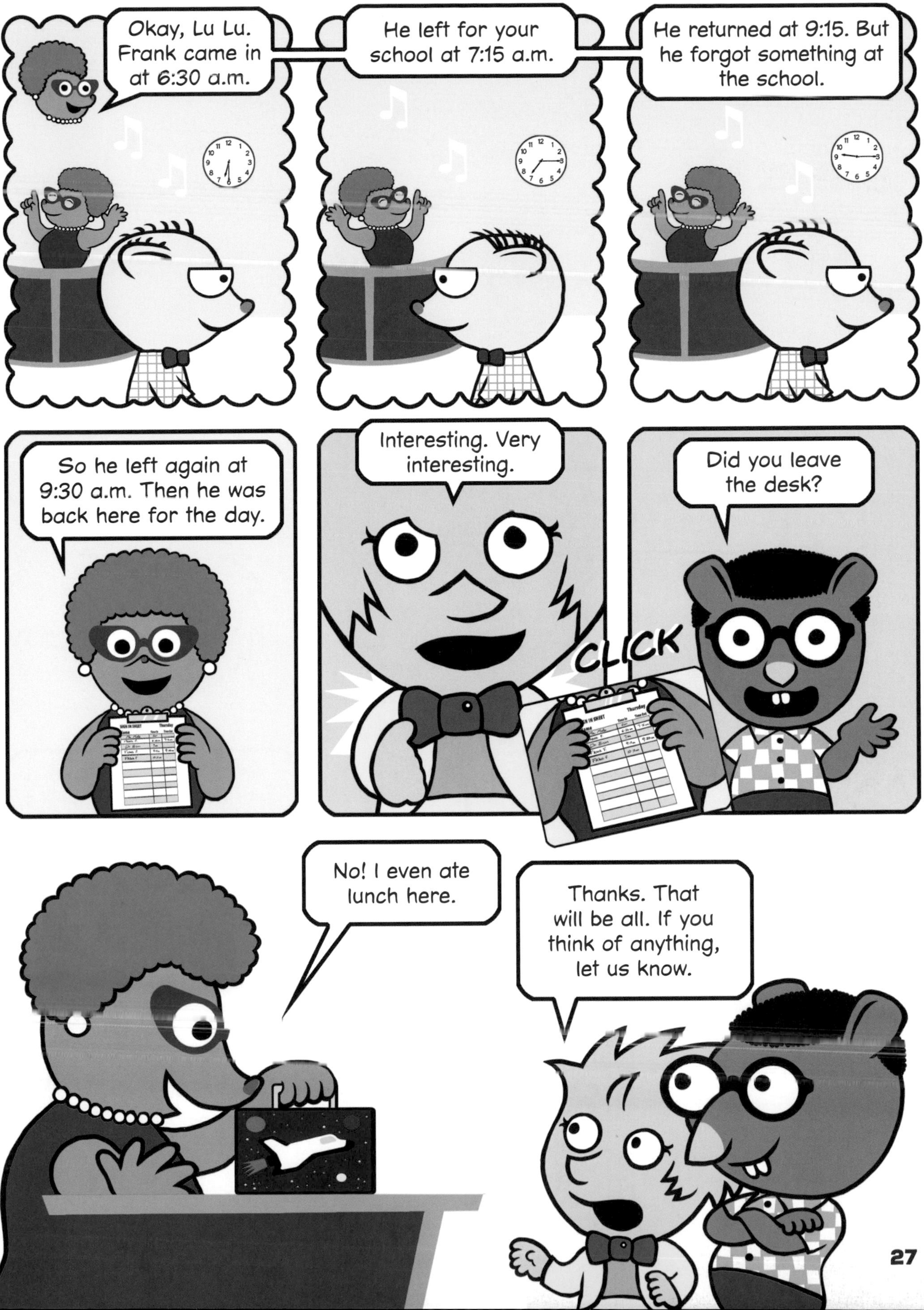
Okay, Lu Lu. Frank came in at 6:30 a.m.
He left for your school at 7:15 a.m.
He returned at 9:15. But he forgot something at the school.
So he left again at 9:30 a.m. Then he was back here for the day.
Interesting. Very interesting.
Did you leave the desk?
CLICK
No! I even ate lunch here.
Thanks. That will be all. If you think of anything, let us know.

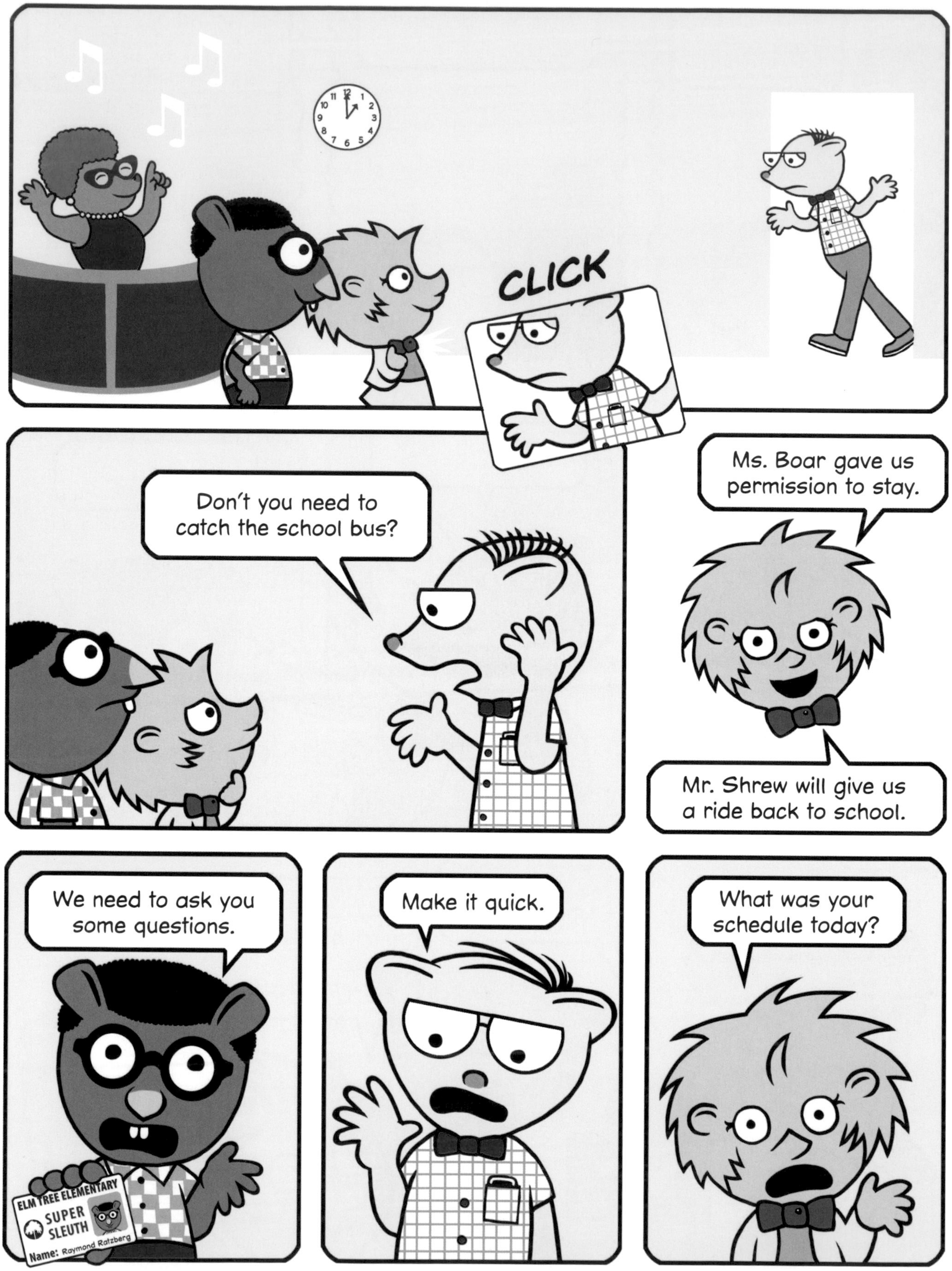
CLICK
Don't you need to catch the school bus?
Ms. Boar gave us permission to stay.
Mr. Shrew will give us a ride back to school.
We need to ask you some questions.
ELM TREE ELEMENTARY
SUPER SLEUTH
Name: Raymond Ratzberg
Make it quick.
What was your schedule today?

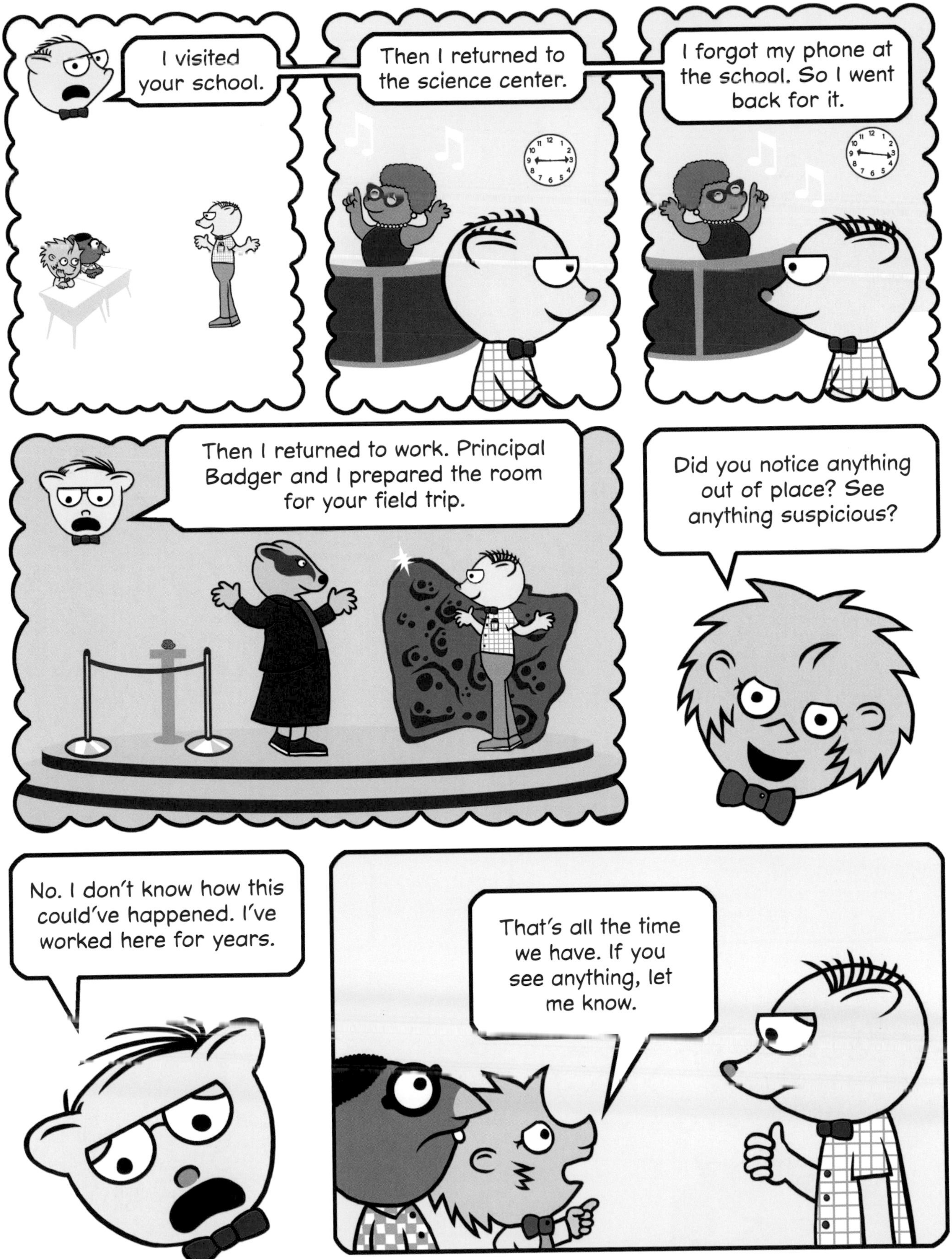
I visited your school.
Then I returned to the science center.
I forgot my phone at the school. So I went back for it.
Then I returned to work. Principal Badger and I prepared the room for your field trip.
Did you notice anything out of place? See anything suspicious?
No. I don't know how this could've happened. I've worked here for years.
That's all the time we have. If you see anything, let me know.

CHAPTER SEVEN
Searching for Suspects

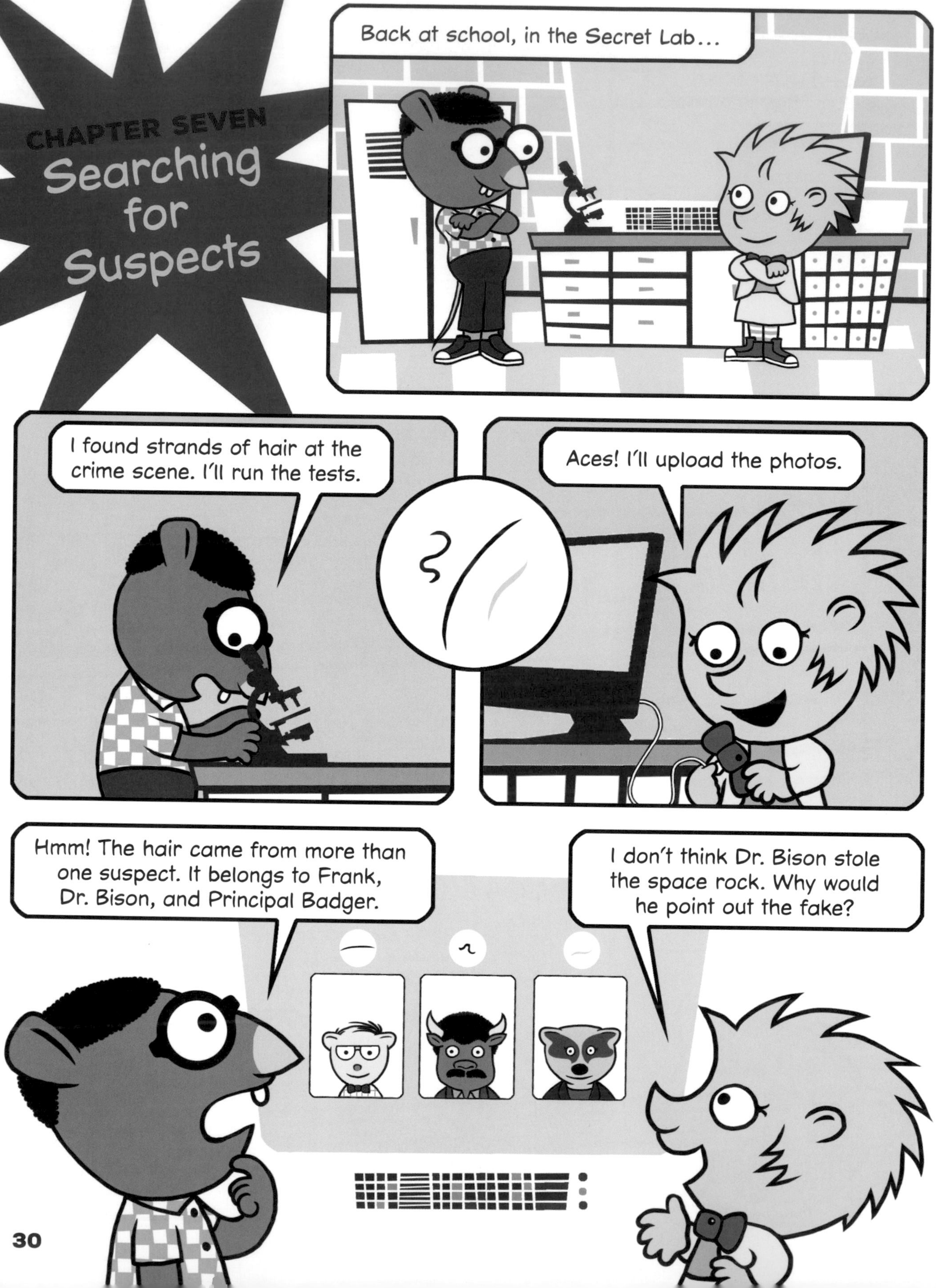

Back at school, in the Secret Lab...
I found strands of hair at the crime scene. I'll run the tests.
Aces! I'll upload the photos.
Hmm! The hair came from more than one suspect. It belongs to Frank, Dr. Bison, and Principal Badger.
I don't think Dr. Bison stole the space rock. Why would he point out the fake?

Indeed. And look what I found *inside* the ropes! Right where they kept the meteorite.

A red button!

This could be an important deet! Who had red buttons?

Oooh! Check it out! This morning, Frank had all the buttons on his shirt. This afternoon, he didn't.

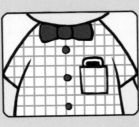

And in between those times, the meteorite was stolen!

Still, we don't know that Frank is the thief.

Principal Badger was near the rock too!

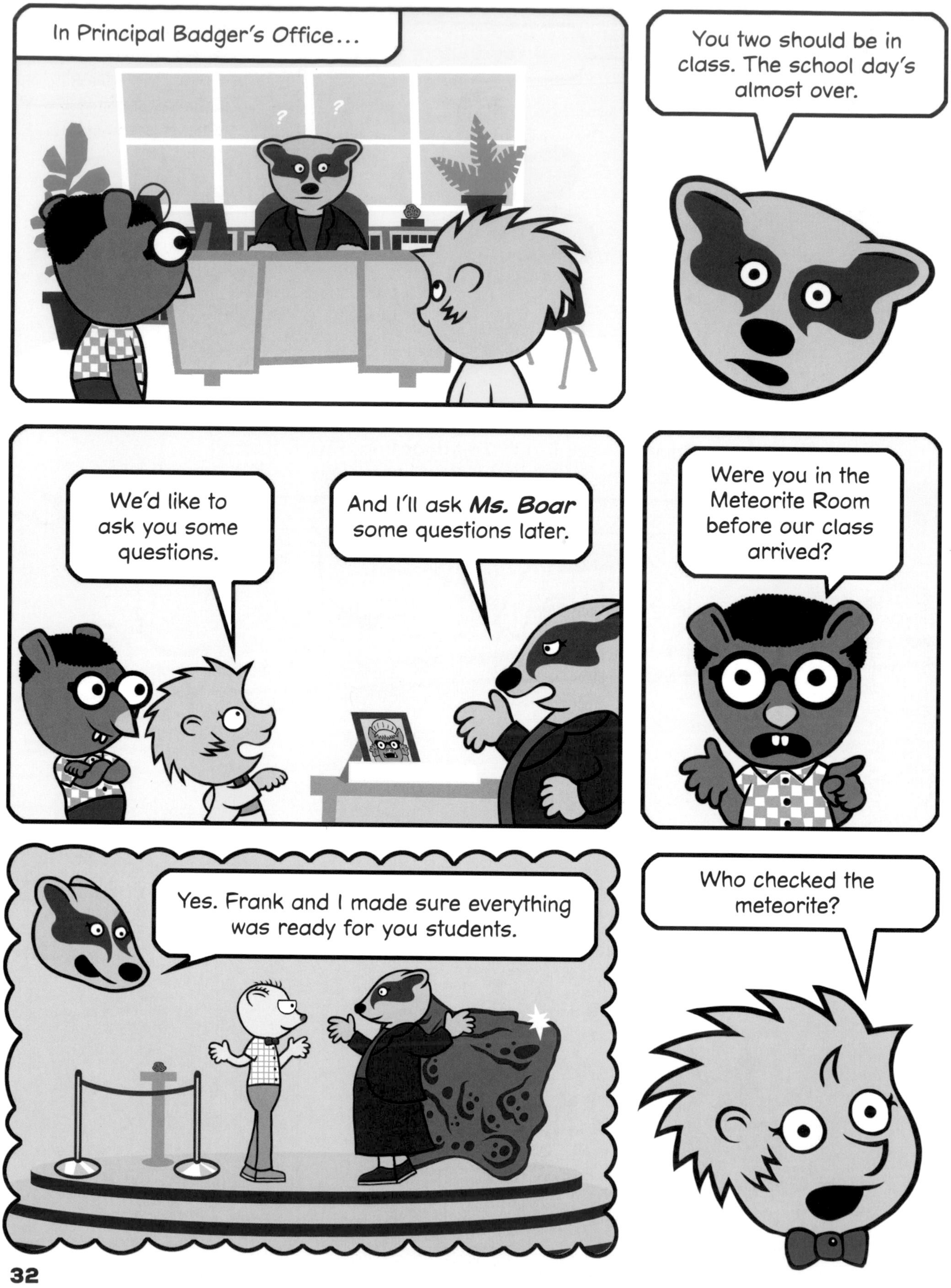
In Principal Badger's Office...
You two should be in class. The school day's almost over.
We'd like to ask you some questions.
And I'll ask ***Ms. Boar*** some questions later.
Were you in the Meteorite Room before our class arrived?
Yes. Frank and I made sure everything was ready for you students.
Who checked the meteorite?

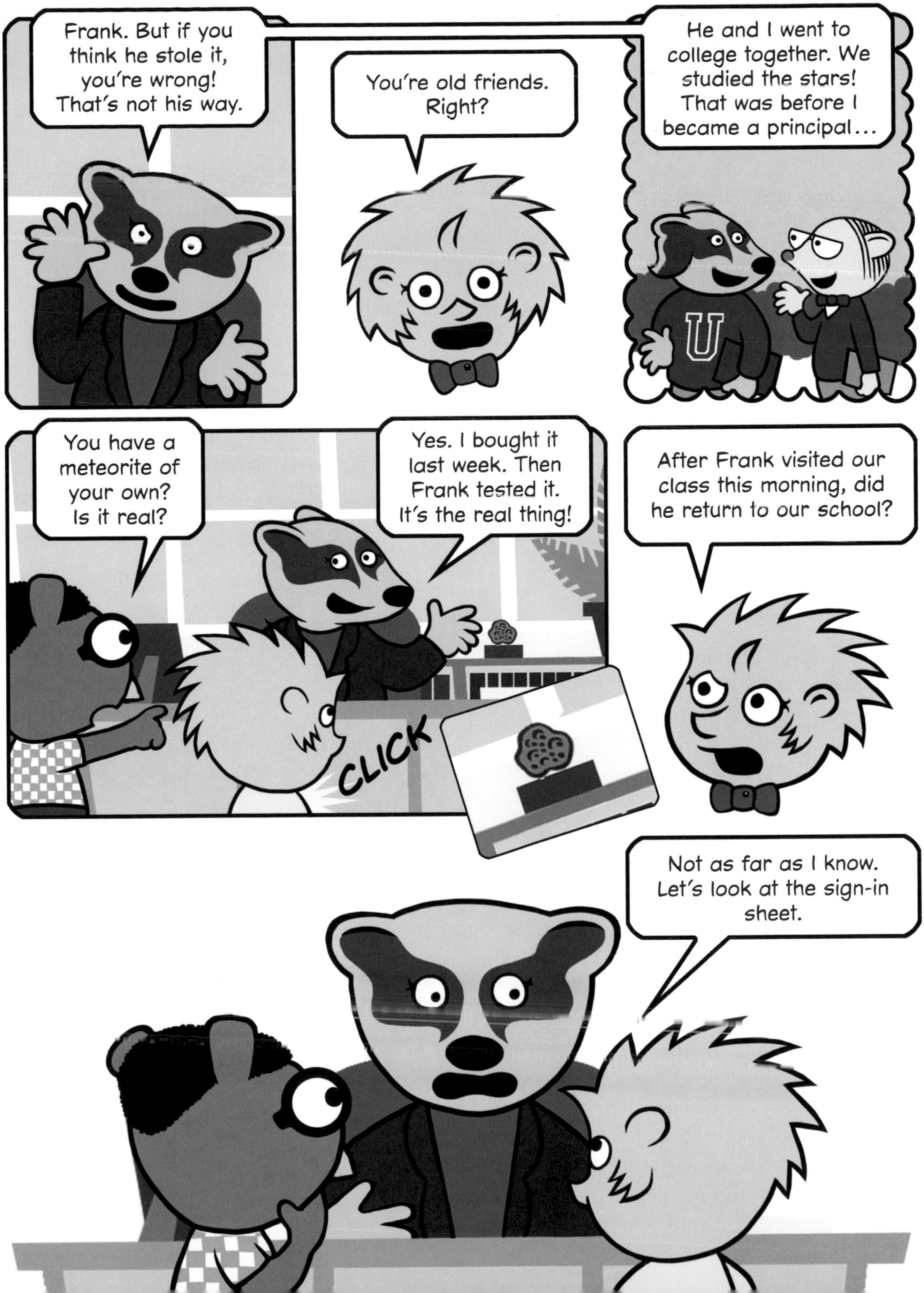
Frank. But if you think he stole it, you're wrong! That's not his way.
You're old friends. Right?
He and I went to college together. We studied the stars! That was before I became a principal...
You have a meteorite of your own? Is it real?
Yes. I bought it last week. Then Frank tested it. It's the real thing!
CLICK
After Frank visited our class this morning, did he return to our school?
Not as far as I know. Let's look at the sign-in sheet.

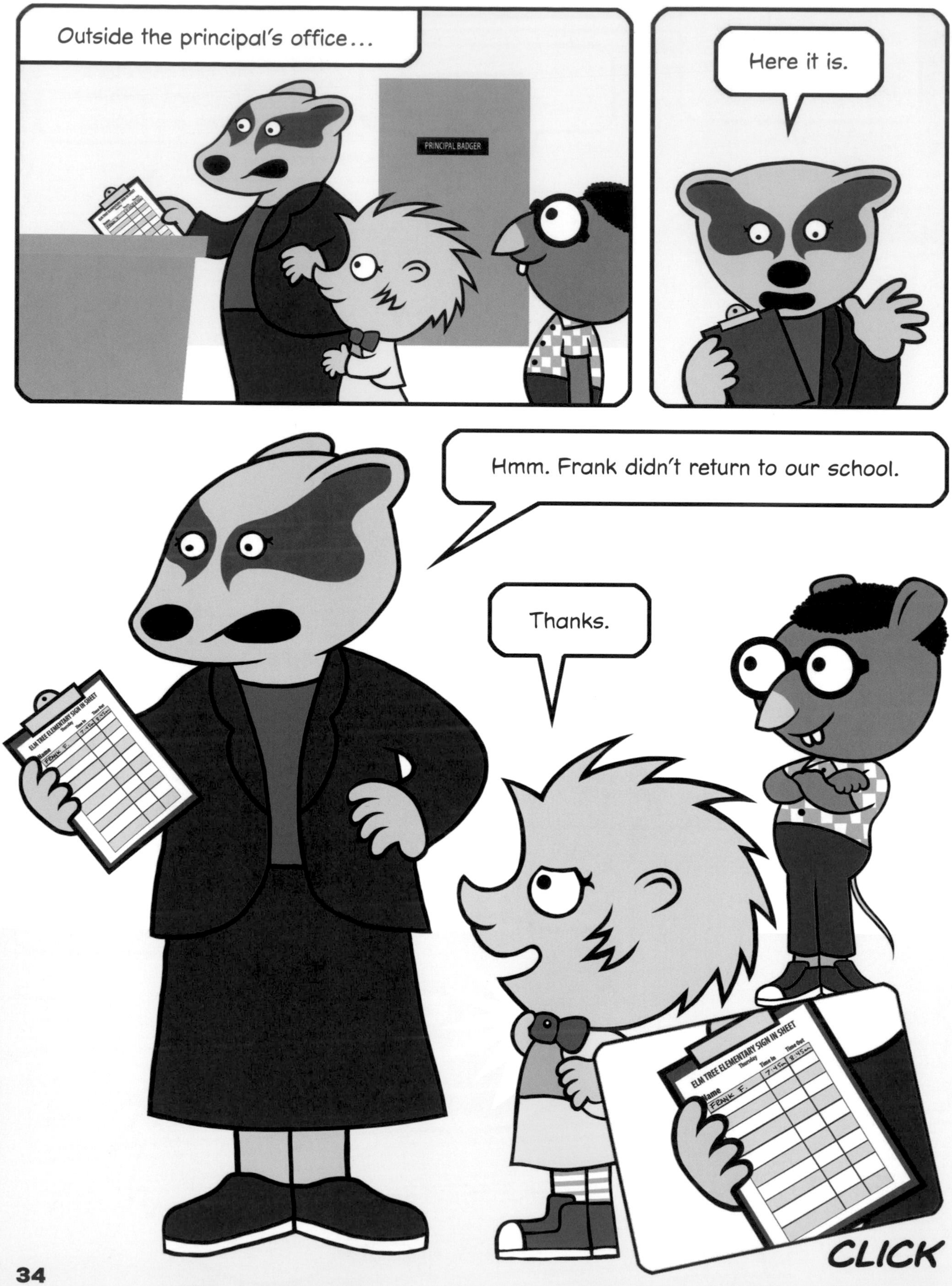
Outside the principal's office...
PRINCIPAL BADGER
Here it is.
Hmm. Frank didn't return to our school.
Thanks.
CLICK

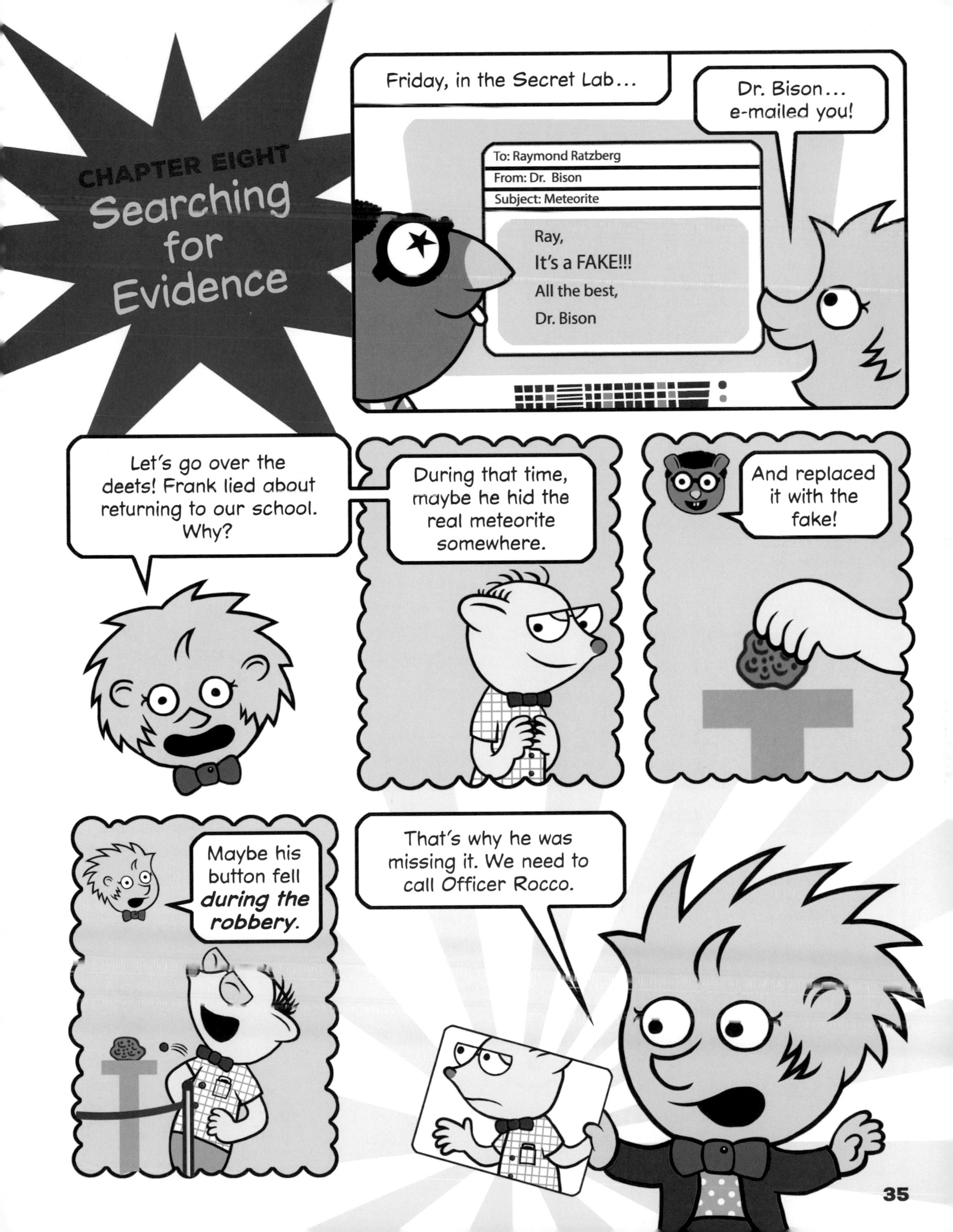
CHAPTER EIGHT
Searching for Evidence
Friday, in the Secret Lab...
Dr. Bison... e-mailed you!
To: Raymond Ratzberg
From: Dr. Bison
Subject: Meteorite
Ray,
It's a FAKE!!!
All the best,
Dr. Bison
Let's go over the deets! Frank lied about returning to our school. Why?
During that time, maybe he hid the real meteorite somewhere.
And replaced it with the fake!
Maybe his button fell ***during the robbery***.
That's why he was missing it. We need to call Officer Rocco.

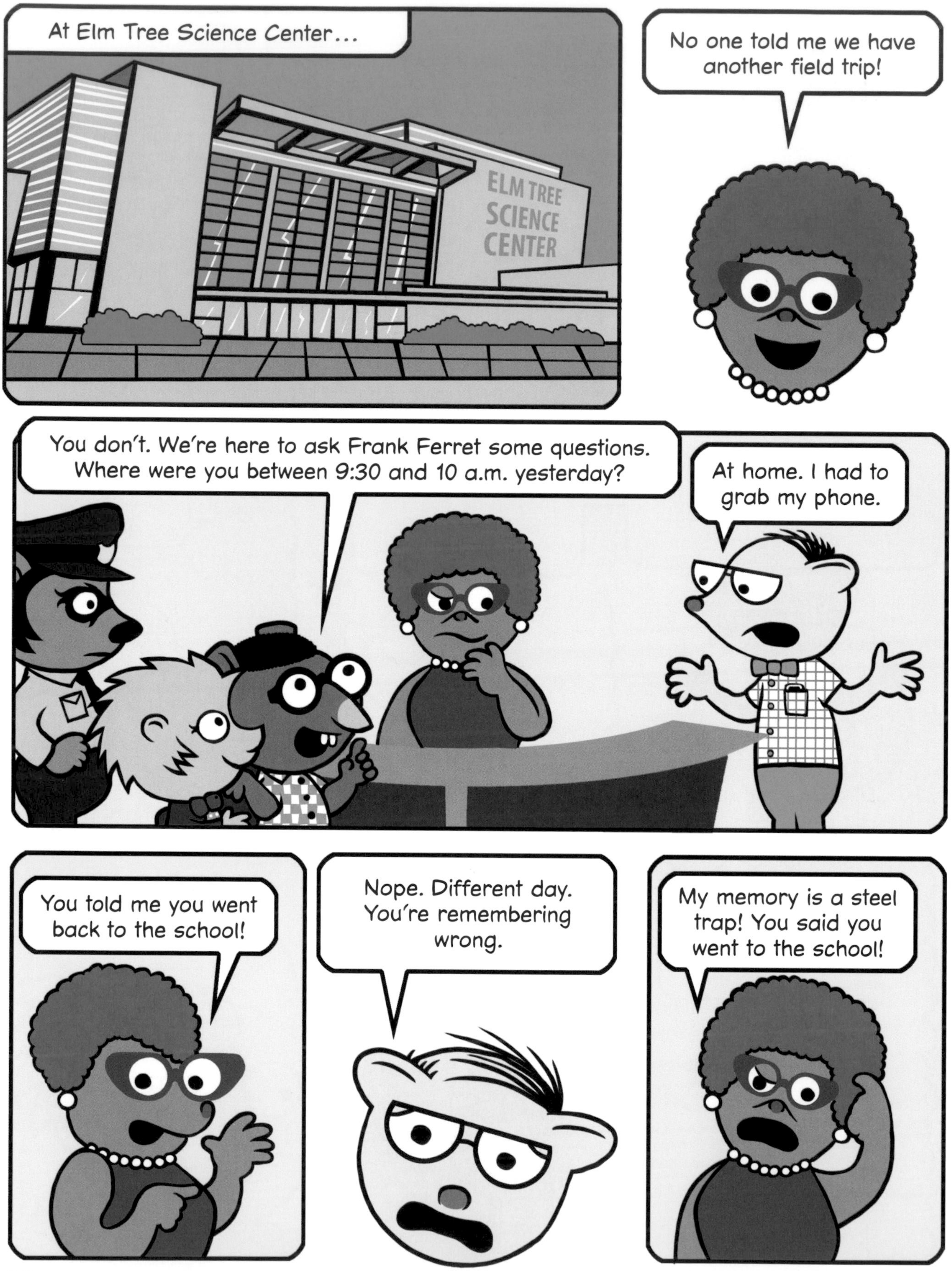

At Elm Tree Science Center...
ELM TREE SCIENCE CENTER
No one told me we have another field trip!
You don't. We're here to ask Frank Ferret some questions. Where were you between 9:30 and 10 a.m. yesterday?
At home. I had to grab my phone.
You told me you went back to the school!
Nope. Different day. You're remembering wrong.
My memory is a steel trap! You said you went to the school!

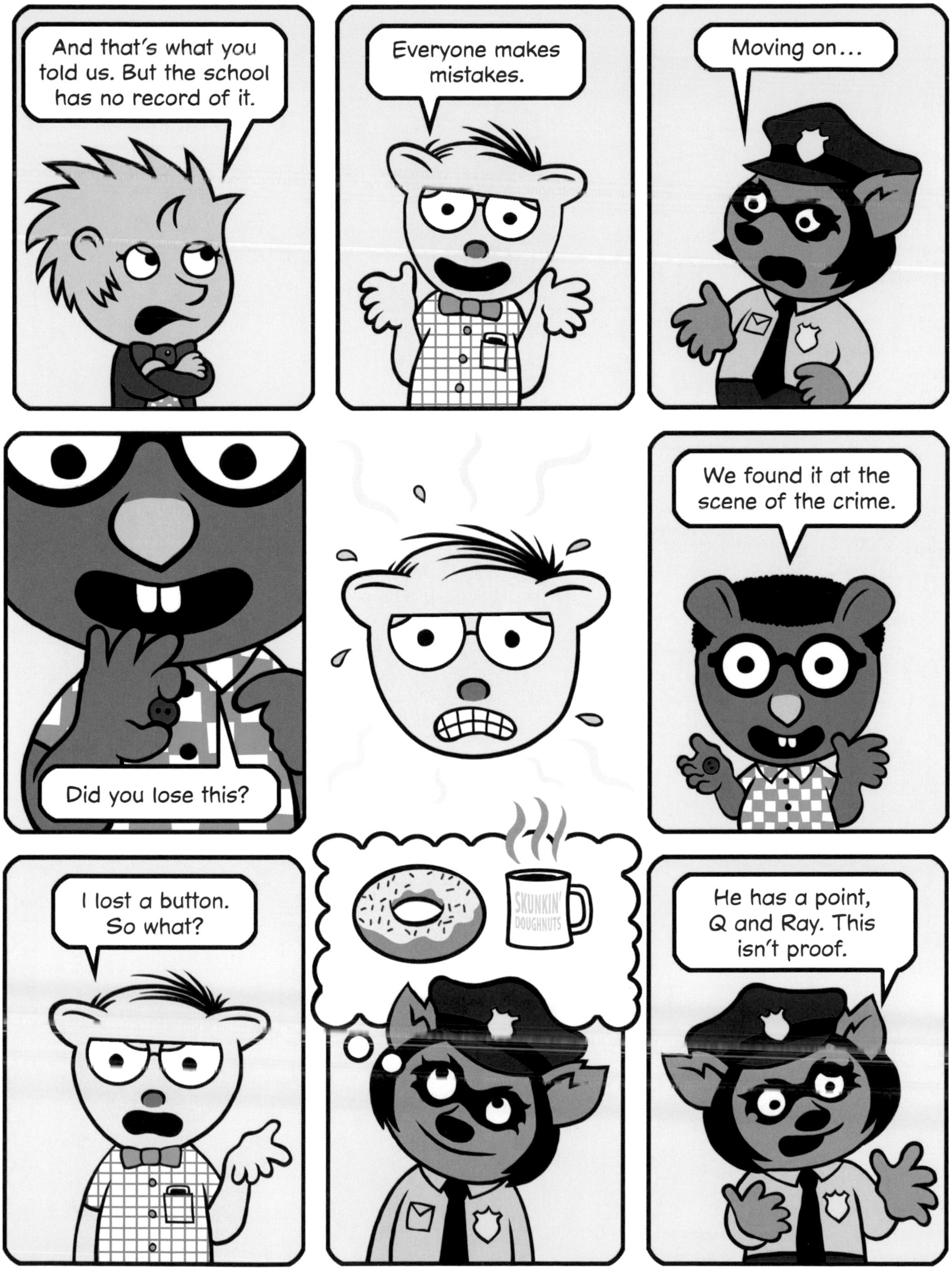
And that's what you told us. But the school has no record of it.
Everyone makes mistakes.
Moving on...
Did you lose this?
We found it at the scene of the crime.
I lost a button. So what?
SKUNKIN' DOUGHNUTS
He has a point, Q and Ray. This isn't proof.

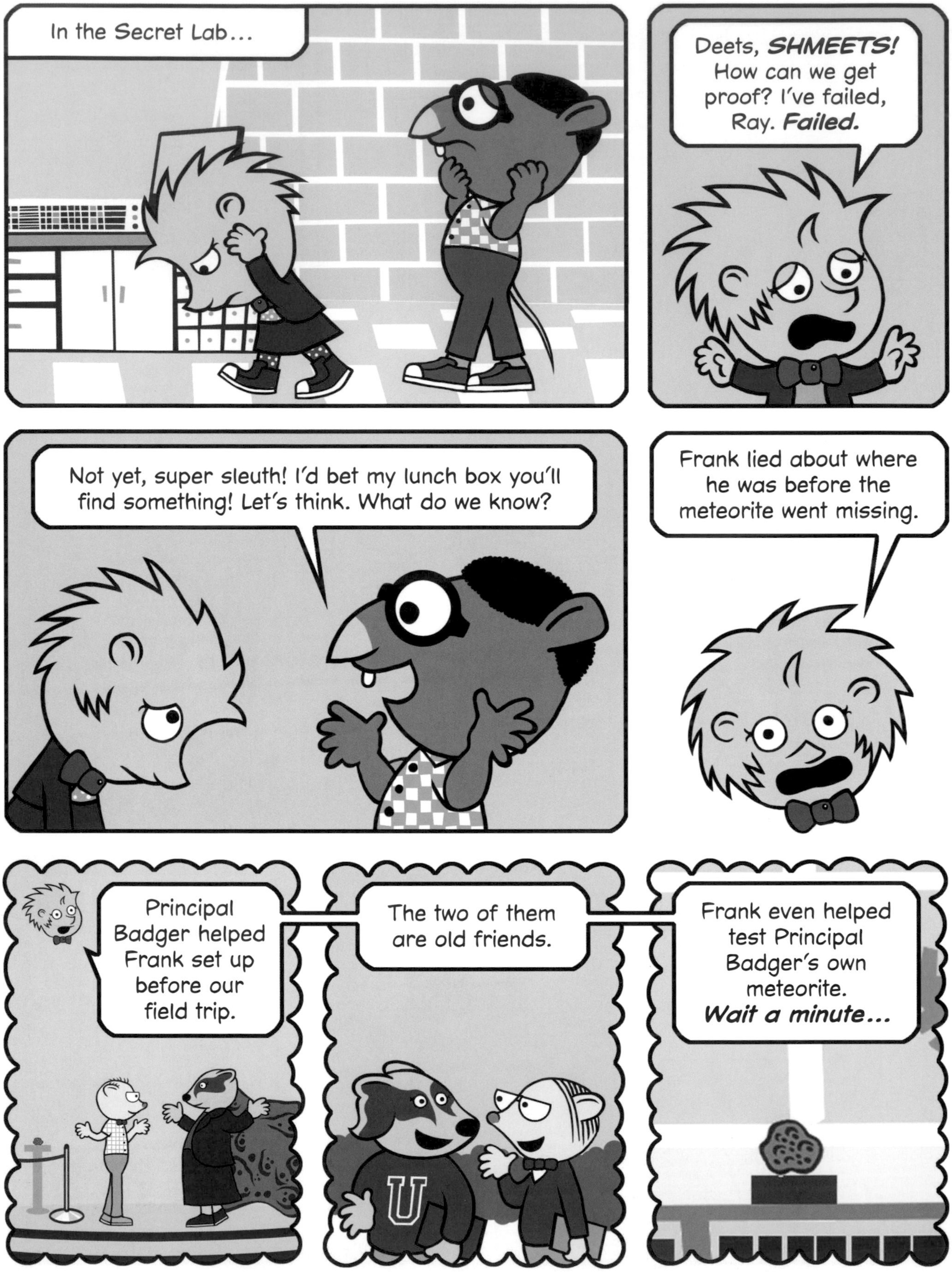
In the Secret Lab...
Deets, SHMEETS! How can we get proof? I've failed, Ray. Failed.
Not yet, super sleuth! I'd bet my lunch box you'll find something! Let's think. What do we know?
Frank lied about where he was before the meteorite went missing.
Principal Badger helped Frank set up before our field trip.
The two of them are old friends.
Frank even helped test Principal Badger's own meteorite. Wait a minute...
U

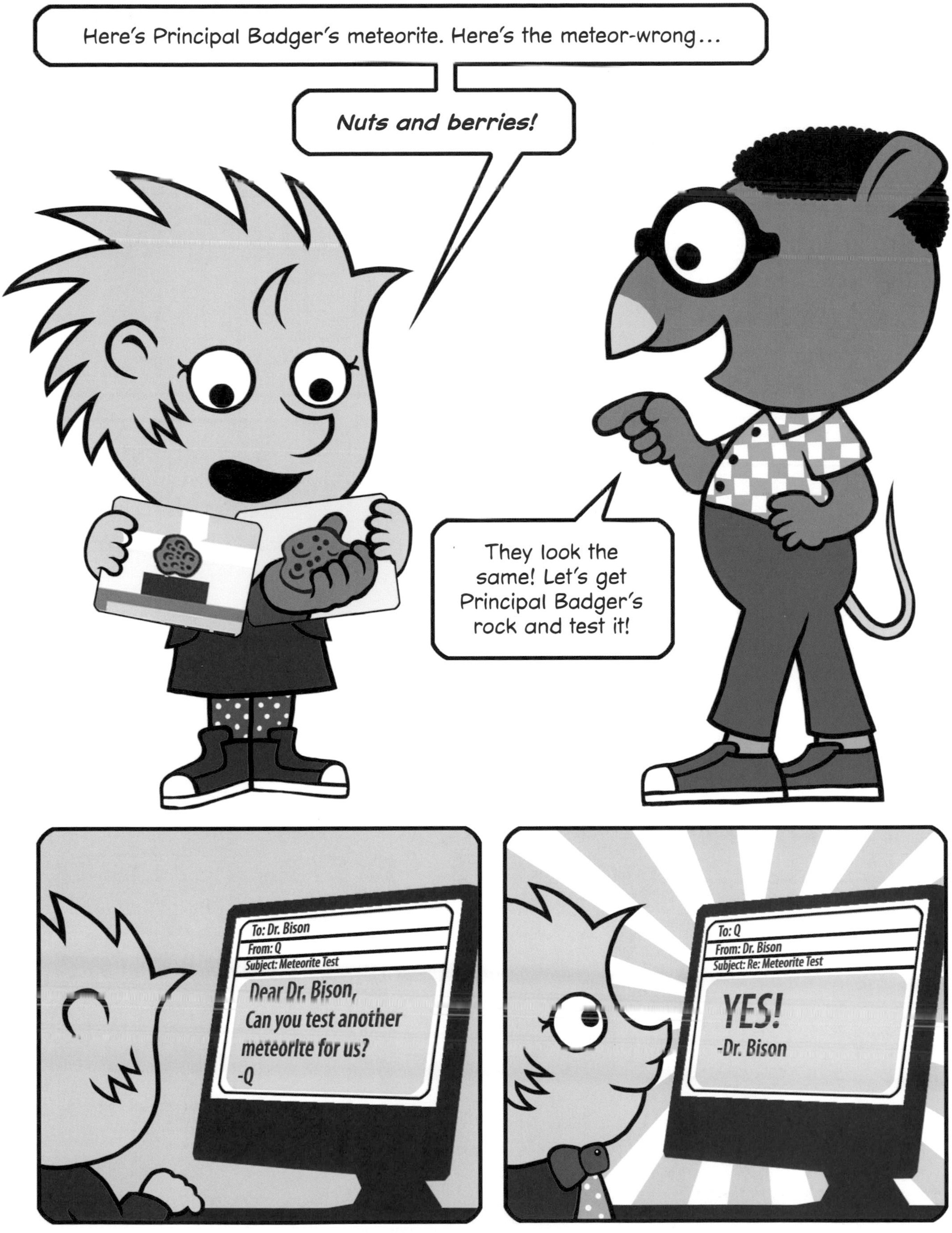
Here's Principal Badger's meteorite. Here's the meteor-wrong...
Nuts and berries!
They look the same! Let's get Principal Badger's rock and test it!
To: Dr. Bison
From: Q
Subject: Meteorite Test
Dear Dr. Bison,
Can you test another meteorite for us?
-Q
To: Q
From: Dr. Bison
Subject: Re: Meteorite Test
YES!
-Dr. Bison

CHAPTER NINE
Rock Stars

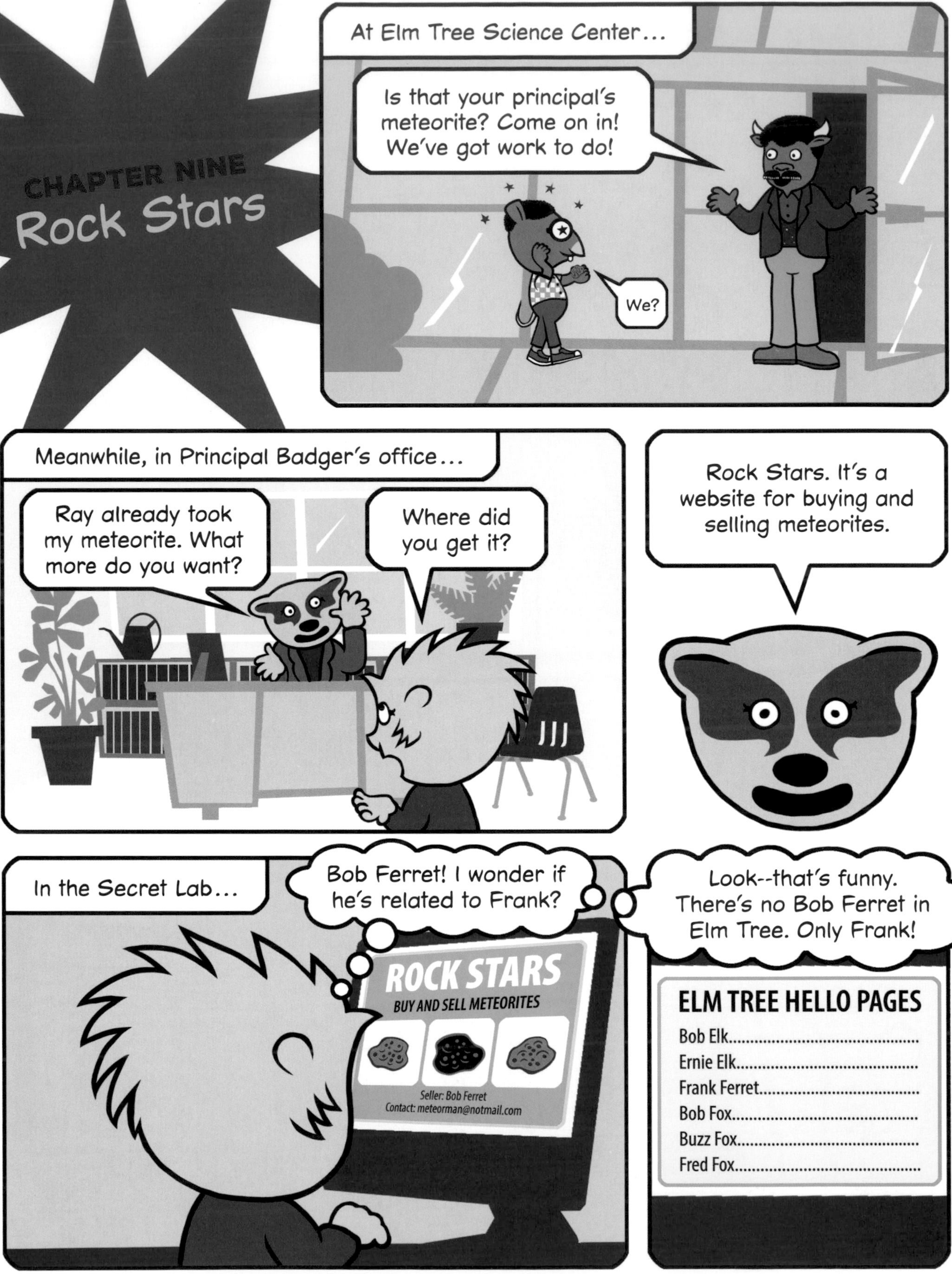

At Elm Tree Science Center...
Is that your principal's meteorite? Come on in! We've got work to do!
We?
Meanwhile, in Principal Badger's office...
Ray already took my meteorite. What more do you want?
Where did you get it?
Rock Stars. It's a website for buying and selling meteorites.
In the Secret Lab...
Bob Ferret! I wonder if he's related to Frank?
ROCK STARS
BUY AND SELL METEORITES
Seller: Bob Ferret
Contact: meteorman@notmail.com
Look--that's funny. There's no Bob Ferret in Elm Tree. Only Frank!
ELM TREE HELLO PAGES
Bob Elk
Ernie Elk
Frank Ferret
Bob Fox
Buzz Fox
Fred Fox

Time to see this guy up close.

To: Ferret
From: Edna
Subject: Buy meteorite?

*Dear Bob Ferret,
I'd like to buy a meteorite.
-Edna*

20 minutes later...

To: Edna
From: Bob Ferret
RE: Buy meteorite?

*Dear Edna,
Great! Let's meet at Skunkin'
Doughnuts. Bring lots of dough.
-Bob*

Time for a disguise!

Near Skunkin' Doughnuts...

At least this Ferret picked a good meeting spot. Where's Q?

SKUNKIN' DOUGHNUTS

It's me. But call me Edna.

Neat-o disguise! I'll follow your lead.

When I raise my hand, move in.

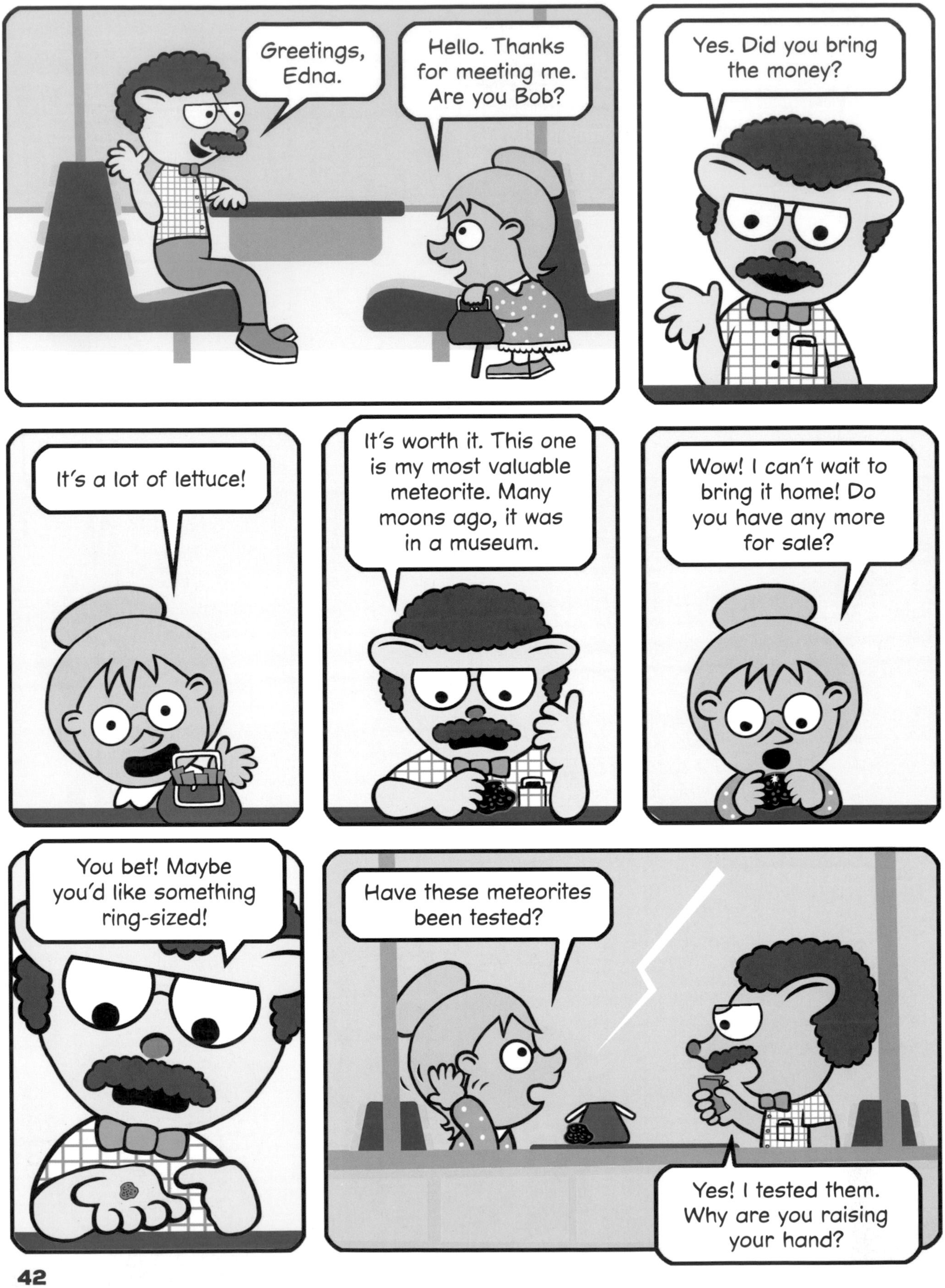
Greetings, Edna.
Hello. Thanks for meeting me. Are you Bob?
Yes. Did you bring the money?
It's a lot of lettuce!
It's worth it. This one is my most valuable meteorite. Many moons ago, it was in a museum.
Wow! I can't wait to bring it home! Do you have any more for sale?
You bet! Maybe you'd like something ring-sized!
Have these meteorites been tested?
Yes! I tested them. Why are you raising your hand?

Hello, Frank. What's with the disguise?

What are you doing here?

Frank, how could you?

This feels like the **Elm Tree Park** Meteorite!

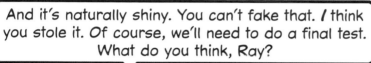

And it's naturally shiny. You can't fake that. *I* think you stole it. Of course, we'll need to do a final test. What do you think, Ray?

Yes... we... test.

It's not the stolen meteorite! I swear!

And what about this small one? It looks like a fake!

I can explain!

We tested Principal Badger's meteorite. And we tested the rock you swapped in for the Elm Tree Park Meteorite. More fakes!

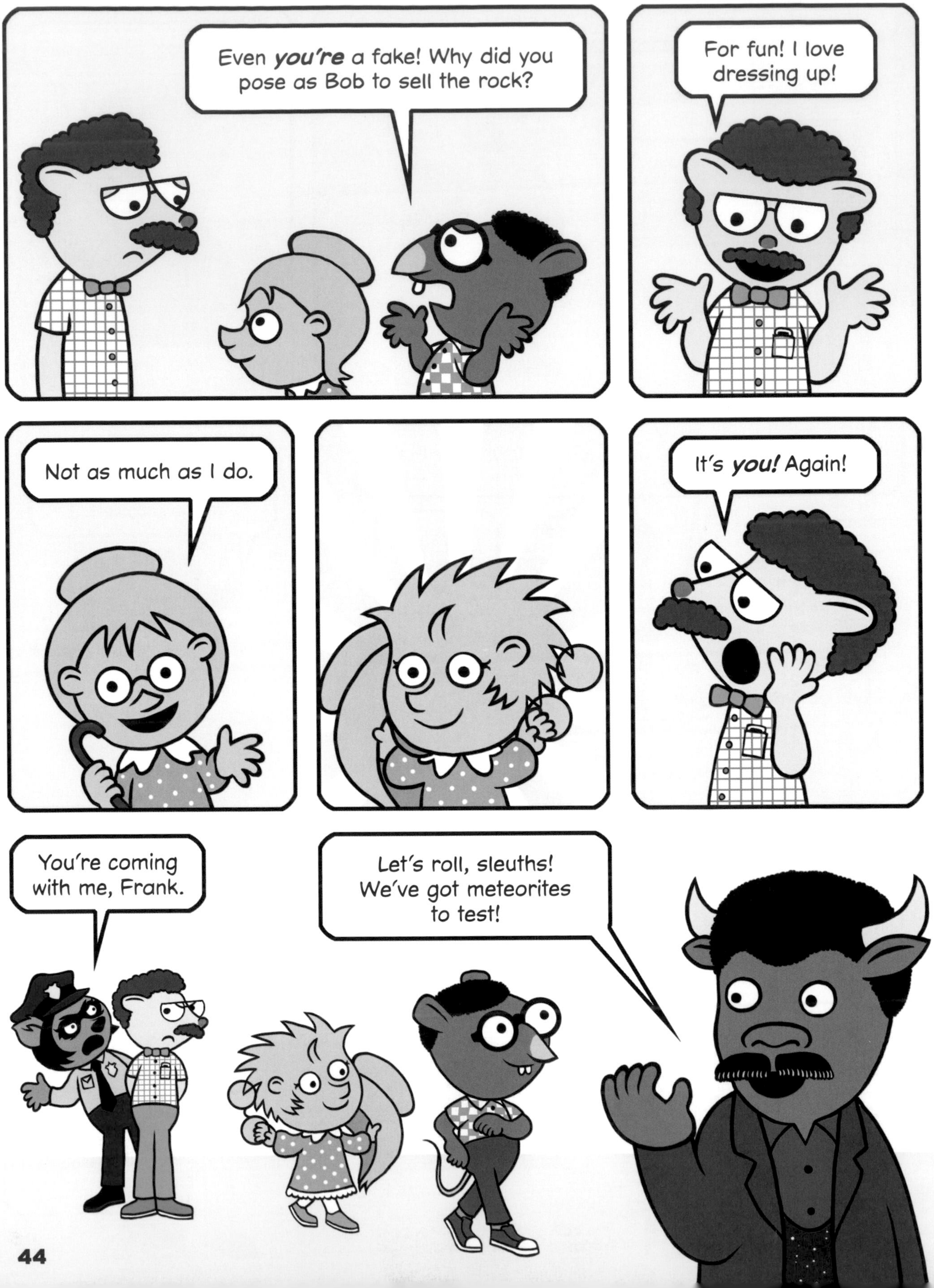
Even ***you're*** a fake! Why did you pose as Bob to sell the rock?
For fun! I love dressing up!
Not as much as I do.
It's ***you!*** Again!
You're coming with me, Frank.
Let's roll, sleuths! We've got meteorites to test!

CHAPTER TEN
A Special Delivery

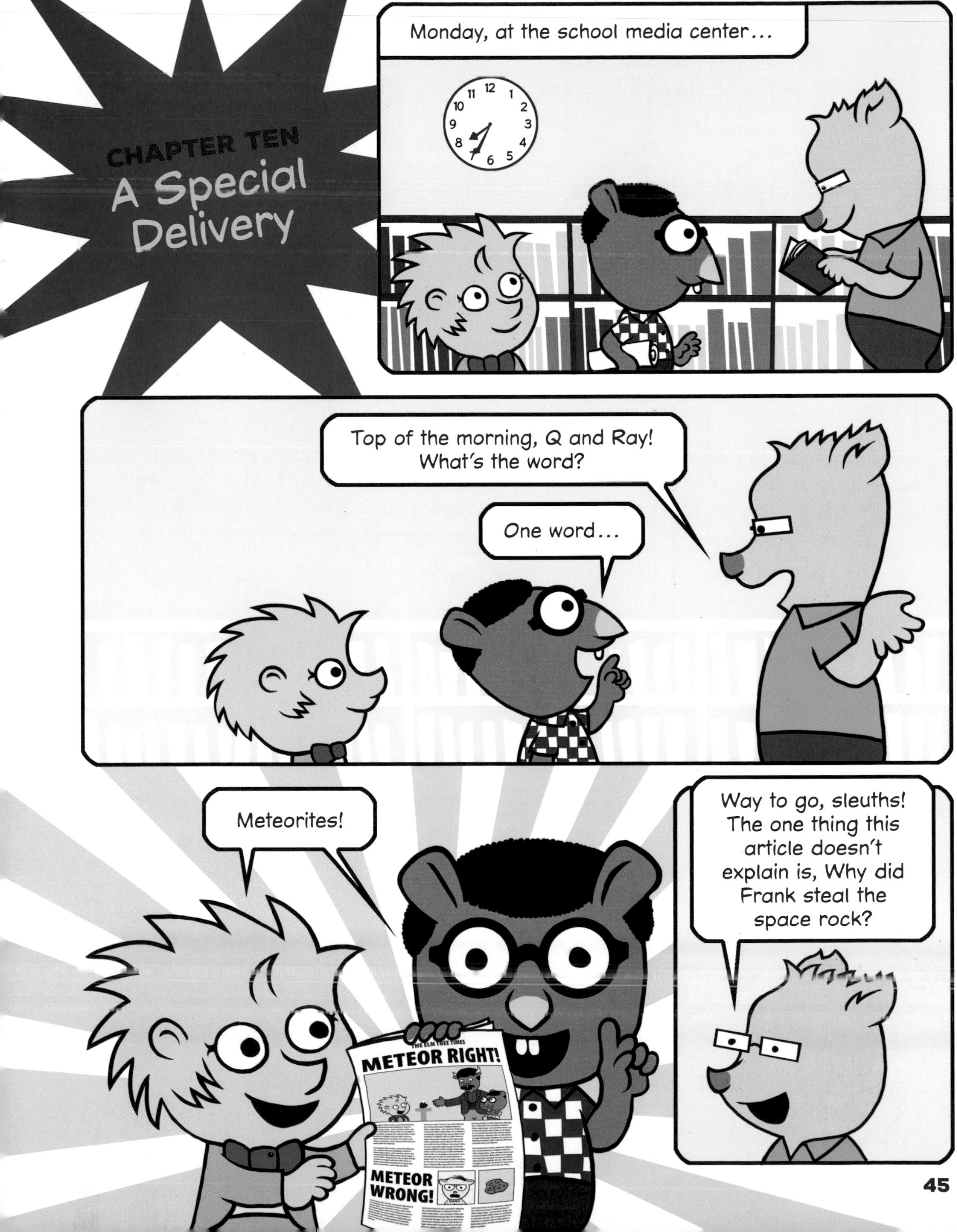

Monday, at the school media center...
Top of the morning, Q and Ray! What's the word?
One word...
Meteorites!
THE ELM TREE TIMES
METEOR RIGHT!
METEOR WRONG!
Way to go, sleuths! The one thing this article doesn't explain is, Why did Frank steal the space rock?

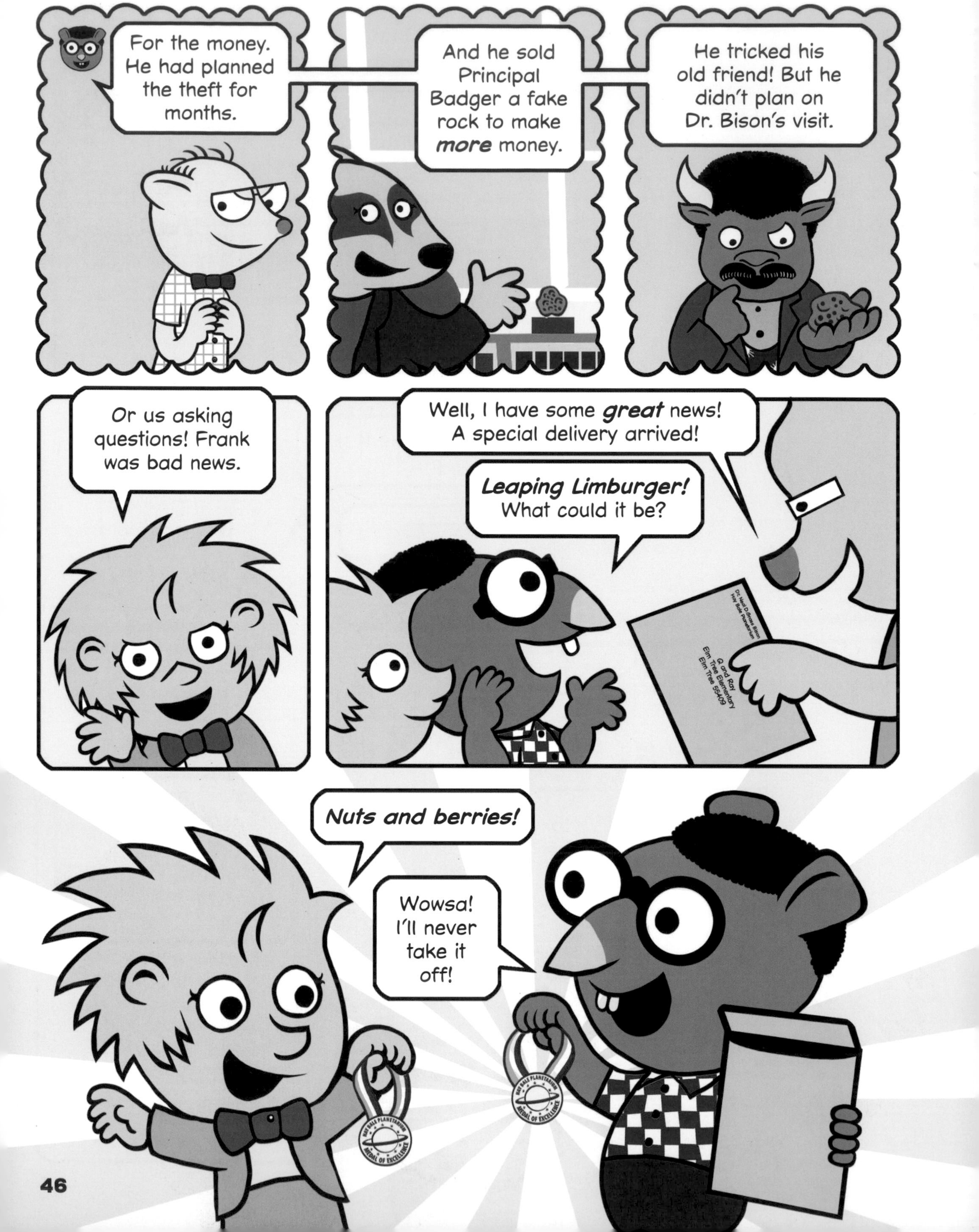
For the money. He had planned the theft for months.
And he sold Principal Badger a fake rock to make *more* money.
He tricked his old friend! But he didn't plan on Dr. Bison's visit.
Or us asking questions! Frank was bad news.
Well, I have some *great* news! A special delivery arrived!
Leaping Limburger! What could it be?
Q and Roy
Elm Tree Elementary
Elm Tree 55409
Nuts and berries!
Wowsa! I'll never take it off!
HAY BALE PLANETARIUM
MEDAL OF EXCELLENCE

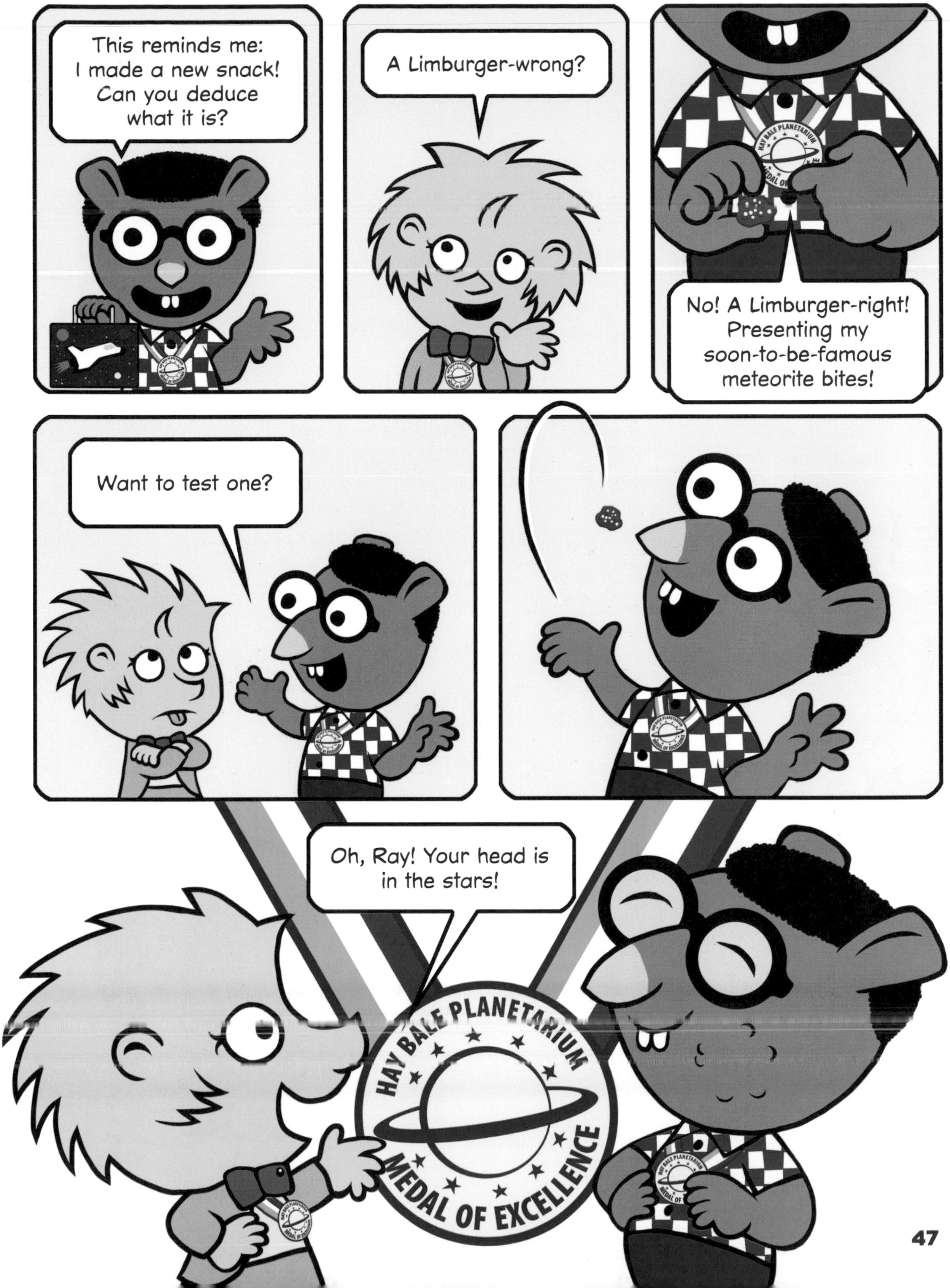
This reminds me: I made a new snack! Can you deduce what it is?
A Limburger-wrong?
No! A Limburger-right! Presenting my soon-to-be-famous meteorite bites!
Want to test one?
Oh, Ray! Your head is in the stars!
HAY BALE PLANETARIUM
MEDAL OF EXCELLENCE

ABOUT THE AUTHOR

Trisha Speed Shaskan has written more than forty books for children, including the Q & Ray series and *Punk Skunks*, both of which are illustrated by her husband, Stephen Shaskan. Several years ago, she watched the Perseid meteor shower and knew someday she'd write a story inspired by it. While writing this book, Trisha loved learning about meteors and meteorites. She hopes you enjoy it too! Visit her at trishaspeedshaskan.com.

ABOUT THE ILLUSTRATOR

Stephen Shaskan is the author and the illustrator of *Big Choo, A Dog Is a Dog, Max Speed, Toad on the Road: A Cautionary Tale,* and *The Three Triceratops Tuff.* He's also the illustrator of *Punks Skunks* and the Q & Ray books. He is super excited to be creating this graphic novel series, since he grew up collecting, reading, and drawing comic books. Stephen and Trisha live in Minneapolis, Minnesota, with their cat, Eartha, and dog, Bea. Visit him at stephenshaskan.com.

FUN FACTS

There's much more information about meteorites to explore! Many meteors don't make it to Earth. They heat up in the planet's atmosphere. Then they vaporize. That means they turn into gas.

Most of the meteorites that do fall to Earth are the size of specks of dust. But even large meteorites are hard to find. People who try to spot them go by the name chasers. Since 1980, only about one meteorite has been discovered in the United States each year.